THE SURGEON'S MEANT-TO-BE BRIDE

BY
AMY ANDREWS

MILLS & BOON®

First published in Great Britain 2006
Harlequin Mills & Boon Limited,
Eton House, 18-24 Paradise Road, Richmond, Surrey TW9 1SR

© Amy Andrews 2006

ISBN-13: 978 0 263 19516 3
ISBN-10:   0 263 19516 3

Set in Times Roman 10½ on 12¾ pt
15-1006-47632

Printed and bound in Great Britain
by Antony Rowe Ltd, Chippenham, Wiltshire

'I'm asking you to let me go so I can find someone who wants a child as much as I do.'

The thought of her with someone else hurt like a fresh bruise deep inside that someone kept prodding. But she was right. If he couldn't give her what she wanted then it was wrong to keep her bound to him.

Gill sighed as he removed the divorce papers from the envelope. 'Are you sure? What we have is pretty special. Are you sure you can find that with someone else?' He didn't mean to sound conceited—he was just stating a fact. And it was buying him time. Putting off the inevitable.

'No, Gill.' She shut her eyes briefly and opened them again. 'I'm just looking for a different kind of love. One that has room for three.'

He nodded slowly at her. Their love had always been kind of all-consuming. Blocking everything and everybody else out.

She looked so lovely standing in front of him, the desire to hold her in his arms was overwhelming.

As a twelve-year-old, **Amy Andrews** used to sneak off with her mother's romance novels and devour every page. She was the type of kid who daydreamed a lot and carried a cast of thousands around in her head, and from quite an early age she knew that it was her destiny to write. So, in between her duties as wife and mother, her paid job as Paediatric Intensive Care Nurse and her compulsive habit to volunteer, she did just that! Amy lives in Brisbane's beautiful Samford Valley, with her very wonderful and patient husband, two gorgeous kids, a couple of black Labradors and six chooks.

Recent titles by the same author:

CARING FOR HIS CHILD
MISSION: MOUNTAIN RESCUE
THE NURSE'S SECRET SON
EARTHQUAKE BABY
THE MIDWIFE'S MIRACLE BABY

THE SURGEON'S MEANT-TO-BE BRIDE

To Mark. For everything.
LUVVM

CHAPTER ONE

0700 HOURS

THE divorce papers burnt a hole in her hand as she carried the large yellow envelope to her soon-to-be ex-husband's sleeping quarters. Nausea threatened and she swallowed hard to dispel it.

Just knock on the door, hand it over, then leave, Harriet lectured herself as her rubber-soled shoes squeaked loudly on the aged linoleum in the hushed corridors. Do not stop for a chat. Do not go in for coffee. Do not let him make love to you.

She tossed her head and clamped down on the irony that threatened to bubble up in her chest and escape as sarcastic laughter. Sex, Harriet. Have sex with you. Their days of love-making were long past and she couldn't afford such romantic stupidity.

They were getting divorced. The end. *Finito.* Period. They were just having a little difficulty remembering their differences in the haze of lust that descended upon them every time they got a little too close. Harriet hadn't yet worked out the co-ordinates of that invisible line—the one that separated close and too close—but she certainly knew when she'd crossed it. Except by then it was usually…always…too late.

Harriet stopped in front of his door, gathering her courage. Tomorrow. She gripped the envelope tighter. She would be gone tomorrow and his signature would be on the papers and she could get on with her life. So she had to do this now.

She'd had the papers since she'd arrived in this country over two months ago but part of her had held back. Somewhere inside there had still been a small kernel of hope. A little Pollyanna ray of sunshine that had believed she could truly convince him to change his mind.

But two months of alternating between fly-by-the-seat-of-your-pants medical drama and snatched moments of incredible can't-get-enough-of-you sex hadn't resolved anything. Sex they were great at. Marriage they weren't.

Harriet took a moment to tie her wavy hair back in a hastily constructed ponytail. He was going to look all messy-haired and sleepy and sexy as hell, so she desperately needed to look no-nonsense. And he hated her hair tied back, and for this task she needed him to hate her a little.

Harriet knocked on the door. The noise echoed loudly down the corridor and she hoped she hadn't woken anyone else. All the surgical teams had been up until 1 a.m. and she didn't think they'd appreciate such an early wake-up call. But this had to be done. She'd put it off too long already.

She heard a mumbled expletive on the other side of the door and smiled to herself as she pictured Gill emerging from under his pillow, staring at the clock and frowning. Please, put a shirt on, she begged silently.

The door opened abruptly and Harriet was confronted with his magnificent naked chest. She looked into his grumpy face and watched as he bit off a retort and a slow lazy smile warmed his sleepy face. Oh, hell! Of all the men in all the world she had to marry one that looked like a naughty angel.

'Harry,' he murmured.

His morning voice stroked across her skin, sending every nerve ending in her body into a frenzy. She knew where the line was today. And she was standing on it.

'I'm sorry I woke you,' she said, lifting her eyes off his smooth pectoral muscles and trying to shut down her peripheral vision so she couldn't see the bulge of his naked biceps.

'I'm not,' he said.

Harriet frowned at him. He lifted a hand and caressed the St Christopher hanging from the delicate silver chain around her neck. He had a mouth that was made for kissing and Harriet could feel herself teetering on the line. She wanted to lean forward and draw his soft bottom lip into her mouth and bite it.

She could feel his gentle tug on the necklace drawing her into the room. Harriet resisted. She knew that crossing the line was not what this was about. Give him the papers and go. Run like the wind.

Harriet brought the envelope up between them, abruptly displacing his hand.

'What's this?' he asked, a small smile playing on his lips and dancing in his grey eyes.

'Divorce papers,' she said, and felt stronger just saying the words.

Gill stared for a moment and shot her another slow smile as he took the envelope from her. He tossed it over his shoulder and Harriet heard it land on the floor behind him.

'Gill...' she chided softly. 'I need you to sign them. It's time.'

He stood to one side and gestured her into the room with a flourish of his deft surgeon's hands.

Harriet shook her head vehemently. 'No.' She knew what would happen if she put her foot over the line. His quarters were three metres by three and dominated by an unmade bed and an undressed man.

'Harriet,' he sighed, but she could see the sparkle of amusement lighting his eyes. 'I'm not going to discuss our divorce with you in the corridor.'

His rich, deep voice oozed like warm chocolate, coating her in its sweet, sticky web. He held out his hand to her. It sounded so reasonable. She looked behind her at the empty hallway and hesitated briefly, before taking his hand and feeling the gentle tug pulling her over the line.

When he reached behind her and pulled her hair free she didn't protest. Neither did she when he kissed her. In fact, she welcomed it greedily, ready to join in this dance they did so well, eager to be naked with him one last time.

Harriet had felt the pull the moment he had opened the door and had known deep inside that resistance was useless. She could pretend as much as she liked that it was over between them, but she knew this would never be over. This insane lust that had blinded her with its ferocity for seven years.

He'd sign the papers and their union would be broken, but this endless urge to be with him, to know him carnally every time they were together, could never be broken. Her only hope was distance. Come tomorrow she was staying the hell away from him—for ever!

Harriet felt a quiver low in her abdomen as the sheer hunger and force of his kiss had her clinging to his broad naked shoulders. She heard him groan her name into her mouth and she whimpered in response.

'Harry,' he said again, tearing his mouth away and looking searchingly into her eyes as his breath came in harsh gasps, his grey eyes stormy with passion.

She claimed his mouth quickly, empowered by his almost bewildered look. The fact that she could do to him what he did to her was a powerful aphrodisiac and she felt her kiss become wild and savage against his full lips. Just for one last time she wanted him to realise what he was turning his back on.

Her hands roamed to the smooth muscles of his chest, trailed down his flat abdomen, and she took pleasure in their quick response to her touch. She could feel them contract beneath her nails and when she slipped her hands beneath his boxer shorts to grab handfuls of his tight buttocks she grinned in triumph as the hardness of his erection pushed urgently between her hips.

Gill grasped the bottom of her scrubs top and whipped it over her head in a swift movement. He didn't bother fumbling with her bra clasp but yanked the cups aside, freeing her breasts and roughly stroked his thumbs over her nipples until they peaked into hard nubs.

He pushed her backwards and she fell against the rumpled bed. Harriet had a moment of clarity when she realised how she must look. Half-naked, her hair spread in wild abandon against the sheets, her bra ripped aside, her breasts achingly aroused. Then Gill removed his boxers and all rational thought fled.

He stood for a moment tall and proud, just looking at

her with more lust than she'd known existed in the whole world. He wasn't embarrassed by his arousal and already she wanted to feel its silky smoothness in her hands, her mouth, deep inside her.

She licked her dry lips and noticed Gill's eyes widen at the unintentional come-on. He reached down and pulled the cord at her waist that held her scrubs up and yanked both them and her undies down in one swift movement. Now she lay totally naked before him as he stood before her, and she couldn't stop the whimper of need that escaped her mouth or holding her arms out to him in silent consent.

And then his weight was on her and his mouth was everywhere. Drawing wet circles around her breasts and sucking her nipples to tortured peaks, nibbling her earlobes, tickling her stomach and licking inside her until she thought she would faint from the need.

And then when the desire built to fever pitch his mouth claimed hers and he let his fingers do the walking. They stroked and caressed and danced their way all over her body, and when he put them deep inside her she had to bite hard on her lip to stop the scream. Even crazed with lust, she remembered how thin the walls were!

'Now,' she whispered urgently, clinging to his neck as his fingers wove a magical rhythm and she could feel her orgasm rushing out from deep inside her, threatening to engulf her at any second.

Their gazes locked as he plunged inside her. Each stroke hurtled her closer, at each stroke his eyes seemed to dare hers to close. She refused. She would not look away or shut her eyes, even as the pressure built. She wanted to look straight at him as she came. She wanted to watch his eyes as he came, too. She wanted their last time to be indelibly imprinted on her retinas. She wanted to see his face as he lost control inside her.

Harriet bit down on her lip as the first wave broke against the shore.

'Say it. I want to hear you,'

The demand was magnified by his panting breaths, trying to hold off his own pleasure until she'd reached nirvana as well. Harriet shook her head. If she let it out, the earth would shake and the parrots in the sparse trees outside would lift in noisy flight and every doctor and nurse in the complex would be woken from their slumbers.

'Let it out,' he demanded again.

She shook her head again and tried to internalise the orgasm that was eroding the edges of her endurance.

'I want to hear you,' he said. 'One last time, Harry. Let me hear you.'

Harriet felt the guttural noise move through her from the tips of her toes, gaining momentum until the sheer enormity of it demanded an escape. She held his gaze, noticing the sheen of sweat on his brow, and realised she could stem the noise and the tide no longer.

'Please, Harry.' His voice was halfway between begging and groaning and she knew that she didn't have the power to deny him this one last request. And she wanted to anyway. She wanted to yell and scream like a banshee. She wanted their last time to be memorable, imprinted on his mind for ever. So she let herself go, crying out his name as the tumult of her orgasm flung her into the far reaches of the galaxy.

She vaguely heard his voice joining hers, crying out in abandon as she hovered above the earth, amongst the stars, at one with the beauty of the heavens.

CHAPTER TWO

'THE papers, Gill.'

Dr Guillaume Remy had been enjoying the discon-
nected feeling of being outside his body, letting his mind
drift through the silky tendrils of sexual limbo. In the
strange world between slumber and wakefulness he could
forget about the papers lying discarded on his floor and that
the woman he loved no longer wanted to be with him.

There was only the wonderful haze of pleasure that
reached deep into his bones, making him feel heavy and
weightless all at the same time. A semi-conscious state
halfway between arousal and satisfaction that he wished
they could stay in for ever. He supposed this was the high
that drug addicts craved and thanked his lucky stars he
didn't need to inject anything to attain it.

He just needed Harriet. Oh, sure, he was no novice.
He'd had his share of women with whom he'd experienced sexual pleasure before his marriage, but Harry...it
had never been like this with anyone but her. They were
so perfectly in tune, so intimately in sync, that sex with her
was an addiction he doubted he'd ever manage to control.

They'd been apart for a year but when she'd rejoined his team two months ago it had been as if their separation had never happened. The way she talked and the way she laughed and the way she moved and her smell were as familiar to him as breathing. The way she kissed him, caressed him, touched him was still the biggest thrill he had ever known.

'Gill!' Her voice broke into the fog floating through his brain. He half opened his eyes and watched her pulling on her clothes, hiding her body from him.

'Come back to bed,' he murmured.

There were few things on this earth better than a naked Harriet. Her body was superb…perfect. She had the body and grace of a ballerina. Naturally slender. Toned arms, thighs and calves, flat stomach, long legs, a perky bottom and pert breasts. Her olive skin was blemish-free and the small mole on her left hip was as fascinating today as it had been seven years ago when she had broken all her rules and slept with him after knowing him for three hours.

Her gorgeous wavy hair flowed like a river of molasses down the elegant arc of her back almost to the curve of her buttocks. He had spent many an hour combing his fingers through its heaviness. It was long enough that if she brought it forward over her shoulders it covered both breasts, mermaid-like.

He had a sudden vision of himself as a lust-struck sailor scooping her up from a rocky outcrop, hypnotised by her beauty, and making love to her on a beach as the waves crashed around them. He felt himself twitch and knew that he wanted her again.

'Gill,' she said again, and the note of exasperation in her voice brought him fully out of his fantasy.

Harriet blasted a glare at him that would have vaporised most men, but still he could feel his erection build. If anything, her crankiness was turning him on. He watched her as she realised what was happening to his uncovered anatomy and the look of hunger on her face had him completely ready.

'Come back to bed,' he repeated in a low growl, and he watched the widening of her eyes as temptation flitted across her features and she absently dug her teeth into her bottom lip.

'You know you want to, Harry.'

He knew instantly he had said the wrong thing as he saw the battle end and a look of grim determination set her lips into a thin line.

'For God's sake,' she snapped, 'get dressed and sign the papers.'

Harriet turned her back to him and Gill knew that he had lost her. He sighed and got up, pulling his boxers on.

'You can turn around now,' he said, amused by the rigidity of her back and the way she was impatiently drumming her fingers against her folded arms.

Gill scooped the envelope off the floor and sat on the edge of the bed as Harriet faced him, her arms still folded. They stared at each other for a few moments, not saying anything.

'So this is why you came back to the team after staying away for so long? So you could hand deliver these?'

She felt two spots of colour rise in her face and stain her cheeks. He made it sound so calculating. She shook her head and swallowed the lump in her throat. She would not be shamed by him. 'You're surely not surprised by them?'

'Well, actually, I am. I thought we were getting things back on track. For God's sake, you've rarely been out of my bed.'

'I came to try one last time, Gill. But we've resolved nothing.'

'I love you, Harry. I don't want a divorce. I didn't want a separation. Look me in the eye and tell me you don't love me.'

'This isn't about love, Gill, and you know it. We want different things.'

'A baby.' He sighed. They'd had this conversation about a thousand times in the year before Harriet had walked out.

'Yes, Gill, a baby.'

Gill couldn't think of anything worse if he tried. Except not being married to Harry. They had a great life. They were free to work where they wanted, live where they wanted, travel where they wanted. All with a backpack and a minute's notice. They could make love all night and sleep in till lunchtime. Was there something so wrong with that?

He didn't know a lot about babies but he did know that their lifestyle would have to change drastically. And they'd been having fun, hadn't they? Travelling around the world with the charity organisation MedSurg Aid Abroad, living rough, working hard, changing lives, making a difference.

Seeing places and people and things, both good and bad, that few people ever got to experience in their lives. Touring the world while fulfilling their deep humanitarian beliefs. It was the ultimate lonely planet lifestyle and he didn't want to give that up for nappies and 2 a.m. feeds.

But with the divorce papers in his hands, the reality of the situation was difficult to ignore. Did he really want to lose her over this? Maybe if he compromised?

'Look, I'm not saying I don't ever want a baby…maybe one day I'll feel differently.'

'I'm 35, Gill. I don't have time to wait for you.'

Harriet could be very stubborn. She didn't sugar-coat

anything. If she felt it, she said it. 'Are you sure? You've had a year, Harry. I don't see you pregnant yet.'

He heard her swiftly indrawn breath and wished he could withdraw the words.

'You think I could go off with someone else and have a baby while I'm still married to you? You don't know me at all. Do you?'

So, he had made her angry—well, join the club. Her changing her mind about what she wanted from life had pissed him off, too. 'Well, I thought I used to but, no, these days I don't know you at all. What the hell happened to "No, Gill, I don't want a baby, never, absolutely not, no way. Too many kids in this over-populated world anyway, Gill." What happened to that? So don't blame me if this sudden desire to have a baby makes me think that you'll stoop to anything!'

'You know damn well why the suddenness, Guillaume Remy!' said Harriet, her voice a vicious whisper.

'Because of Rose? Your little sister has a baby and suddenly your clock is ticking louder than a home-made bomb?'

'Don't be so bloody obtuse,' she said through clenched teeth. 'Yes, Rose started it—how could you not want a baby when you look into Tom's beautiful chubby face? But if you can't understand why discovering that I only have one ovary and Fallopian tube could knock me for six, maybe I don't know you either. I'm sorry I changed the plot on you, but when a gynaecologist tells me I might have trouble conceiving, it comes as a bit of a shock. Surely you can see that?'

No, he couldn't. He was a man. And not just that but a man who didn't have a paternal bone in his body. Sure, babies were cute—Tom was very cute. But their appeal had more to do with being grateful he could hand them back than any pleasure he took from holding them.

He'd had a close call as a med student that had scared the hell out of him. There had been no feelings of joy or expectancy, just a horrible sinking feeling that his life was over. He'd carried that experience with him always and in his head babies always equalled the end of your life.

As a doctor he had a great deal of empathy for the plight of the world's poor and starving children and those working like dogs from dusk to dawn and those torn apart by diseases, war and poverty. He admired their strength and resilience and he'd spent many years patching them up when they were hurt or wounded, caught up in adult wars, but he'd never had the desire to adopt any of them or, God forbid, have one of his own.

He had such a strong sense of social responsibility. There was so much he could offer this world. Having kids would just be a distraction from that purpose. His grandfather, who had fought with the French resistance before migrating to Australia after the war, had raised him to think of the plight of others and Gill had always felt immensely proud of the work he did.

But. He was holding his divorce papers in his hand. Before him stood the woman he loved. Who loved him. And she was asking him for something. Was prepared to never see him again, to cut all ties. Was he that strong? Did his career mean more to him than her? Did the world's children mean more to him than the one she so desperately craved?

He sighed. Saying goodbye to Harriet for ever wasn't possible. Being apart from her for a year had been hard, but part of him had felt at ease, unbothered, knowing that it was temporary. That Harriet would get over her problem and come back and they'd continue their lives. But divorce? She was serious.

'Look, OK. You want a baby? All right, then, fine. Let's have a baby.'

He didn't know what he expected but it certainly wasn't Harriet's cool, sceptical gaze. He thought she'd leap into his arms and tear the papers up. Instead, she rolled her eyes and her lips flattened into a terse line.

'Don't do me any favours, Gill.'

He would have been an idiot to miss the sarcasm. 'I mean it, Harry. Really.'

'No, you don't, Gill. You're just trying to appease me. Well, no, thank you very much.'

Hell! What did she want from him? 'Well, don't say I didn't offer,' he said glibly.

'Offer? Offer!' she raged. 'I don't want an offer, Gill. I want you to want a baby with me so much that your breath hurts when you think about it. That your arms ache and your heart feels bereft and your stomach is empty at the thought of not having one. You have to want one with very fibre of your being, Gill. Every cell. Can you offer me that, Gill? Because if you can't then don't try and placate me. It's insulting.'

'Look, OK, you're right. I don't. But I'm still willing to give it a go,' he said quietly.

Harriet sighed. 'How willing? Are you prepared to give up your job, your career, this lifestyle?'

'I could have both,' he said, annoyed at her all-or-noth-ing attitude. 'You could go home and have the baby and I could have two months abroad and one month at home.'

OK, he was just making this up as he went along, but

even he had to admit it sounded terrible. He could hardly blame her for her appalled expression.

'No, Gill. You can't. I don't want to have a baby and be stuck at home by myself for great chunks of time. I want you to *want* to be around all the time for me and the baby. I don't want to have to lie in bed each night worrying that you're going to get shot by a local warlord or die in a helicopter crash or catch Ebola or something. You forget so easily that this work we do is dangerous. I can't live like that.'

'I could maybe cut down to just one or two overseas missions a year…'

He sounded lame and uncommitted. He'd hate it. He'd hate being away from the action so much, and she knew it. 'And how long would we last, Gill? How long before you resented me? Resented the baby?'

Gill swallowed as he thought about her question. What an awful situation that would be.

'This isn't about me forcing you to do what I want. This is me saying I'm sorry, I changed the rules. You didn't sign up for this and I know this isn't what you want. I've always known. Heaven knows, I never expected to feel this way either. I've tried to change your mind but I can't make you want this the way I want it. And I do want it, Gill. I need it. And I'm asking you to let me go so I can find someone who wants it as much as I do.'

The thought of her with someone else hurt like a fresh bruise deep inside that someone kept prodding. But she was right. If he couldn't give her what she wanted then it was wrong to keep her bound to him.

Gill sighed as he removed the papers from the envelope. He could see her fingers stop their drumming and knew she was holding her breath. His eyes fell on the phrase 'irreconcilable differences'. How pertinent. That was exactly their problem. They loved each other. They just wanted different things.

'Are you sure, Harry? What we have is pretty special. Are you sure you can find that with someone else?'

He didn't mean to sound conceited—he was just stating a fact. And it was buying him time. Putting off the inevitable.

Harriet shook her head and he was surprised to catch a shine of tears. 'No, Gill. I'm not sure. I doubt I'll ever love anybody as much as I love you. I honestly believe there's only ever one true love for everyone. But that's OK, I'm not looking for that. I know there's someone out there that can make me happy and give me what I want the most.'

'So you're going to settle?' he asked incredulously.

'No, Gill.' She shut her eyes briefly, blocking his amazement out, then opened them again. 'I'm just looking for a different kind of love. One that has room for three.'

He nodded slowly at her. Their love had always been kind of all-consuming. Blocking everything and everybody else out.

She looked so lovely, standing in front of him, that the desire to hold her in his arms was overwhelming. She pulled a pen out of her scrubs breast pocket as if she'd read his mind, derailing his base urge. Yes, they'd had a good run but now it was time to let her go.

He took it from her and signed at the indicated places in his indecipherable doctor's handwriting next to her neat signature. He placed her copies back in the envelope and handed them back to her, keeping his.

'Thank you,' she whispered.

He nodded and watched as she turned on her heel and left the room.

CHAPTER THREE

IF ANYONE noticed their indifference at the breakfast table, they didn't say anything. In fact, as each of the team joined them at the communal table, good-humoured jokes were told about their early morning wake-up call.

'Hell,' said Joan Sunderland, yawning as she pulled out her chair. Joan was the team's anaesthetist and had been working with MSAA and Gill for ten years. She was English, originating from Liverpool. 'Parrots were loud this morning.'

'Parrots?' said Helmut. He was a Berliner and, as an anaesthetic technician, was Joan's right-hand man. 'Sounded human to me.' And he winked at Harriet.

Harriet blushed and stole a furtive glance at Gill. He was concentrating on his toast but she could see the poorly suppressed grin. There was something so wrong about the team teasing them when Gill had just signed the divorce papers.

But, on the other hand, it was typical. They were a close-knit team. They'd been together on and off for a long time. They performed a stressful job in high-pressure situations and none of them could have come through some of the more awful things without the support of each other.

'Hey, you two, keep it down next time,' said Katya, her flat Russian accent accentuating her renowned bluntness as she and Siobhan entered the room together and joined them, completing the team.

Everyone laughed. Even Harriet managed a grin. She glanced around the table and noticed how relaxed and happy they all were. When Harriet had rejoined the team in their current locale two months ago they had been a little cool towards her. Tense and worried.

After all, they were the ones who had put up with Gill after she had left a year ago and the dreadful year before that when their relationship had slowly crumbled. Apparently his mood had been foul for a long time and, as delighted as they'd been to welcome her back into the fold, they'd been wary about the effect on the team atmosphere.

Cohesiveness was essential in their line of work. They didn't have to all be bosom buddies but it helped. The dreadful security situations they faced in the countries they visited often meant they couldn't even go out and soak up some local culture. They were stuck with each other's company for two months at a time. Harmony was important.

And there was a certain sense of loyalty for Gill. Harriet had felt it the minute she had got back. Nobody had judged her but they'd been through Gill's highs and lows for the previous year and it had been only natural for their sympathies to lie with him.

Gill was also the kind of guy who commanded loyalty and respect. Harriet sneaked another look at him as he poured coffee from the percolator into his mug. In his scrubs the naughty-angel look had gone. He was Dr Guillaume Remy. Surgeon *extraordinaire*. Calm and capable. Brilliant and cool under pressure.

Not a hot-shot arrogant city surgeon, specialising in a glamorous field and making heaps of money but a brilliant general surgeon getting paid a pittance to help the world's poor and needy.

A real team player. A doctor who knew the value of a team and cherished the contribution of everyone. No throwing instruments around theatres and chucking tantrums. He possessed a poise that was exemplary and in-stilled a quiet confidence in all who worked with him.

He brought his mug to his lips and Harriet admired his long, beautiful fingers. She deliberately didn't think of what they'd just done and where they'd just been and how they could stroke against her skin and reduce her to a whimpering mass of need. She thought instead about how many lives they'd saved. How efficient they were with a scalpel. How deftly they accepted an instrument without needing to look. How neatly they could suture to keep scarring to a minimum.

Her gaze travelled up to his face and lingered there for a while. His grey eyes were clear and bright, like a still tranquil pond, and his fine sandy hair framed a face that could almost be described as beautiful.

He looked…European. Tall with finely chiselled features, fabulous cheekbones and a regal nose. His body was lean, fine-boned, and had she not known him at all, his French heritage would not have surprised her. Yes, he was an Australian through and through, but there was just something so French about him also…

He laughed at something Helmut had said and Harriet blinked, realising she was staring. She tuned back into the conversation and immediately picked up the undercurrent of excitement as they all contemplated their last day of the mission. Tomorrow morning the organisation would fly them to London and then on to their different corners of the world for a month's R and R before bringing them together again in another unfortunate part of the planet.

They were doing their things-I-have-missed-most-about-home routine. Yes, they all loved their jobs sometimes with an almost fanatical zeal, but two months away from all you knew and loved, flung into the pressure cooker of a crumbling foreign nation, it was only natural to miss certain things. It was a game they always played on the last day of a mission. There was only one rule—it had to be something different every time.

'A BBQ and my grandfather's *escargots*,' said Gill.

Hmm, thought Harriet. Now, that she could relate to. Henri cooked the best snails. They were addictive.

'The zoo. And frozen cobwebs,' said Helmut.

Well, living in Sydney, she didn't see too many frozen anything but she understood the sentiment. In this place it didn't even get cool overnight. Just the same oppressive heat. No wonder the locals were so crazy. If she had to live here permanently, she'd want to kill somebody, too.

'Ice-skating and vodka. The proper stuff,' said Katya. Everyone laughed, no doubt remembering the time they'd all got merry together at an airport stopover a few years back on Katya's vodka when their plane had been delayed.

'The Mersey and British Rail,' said Joan, and laughed at her own joke.

'Well, I'm going to say shopping in the high street and the smell of peat fires,' said Siobhan in her lilting Irish accent.

Harriet and Gill had stayed a few days at Siobhan's family's farm deep in the Irish countryside five years ago, and she'd loved the earthy smell of burning peat as well. Harriet smiled fondly at the memory and it took her a few seconds to register that they were waiting for her contribution.

She glanced at Gill and quickly looked away as she met his steady grey gaze. What she missed most about home was the beachfront apartment she and Gill lived in at Bondi, and how they would make love all night and sleep till noon, then stroll along past all the cafés and eat pasta at their favourite Italian one. She missed that a lot.

'Mangoes.'

She smiled as an unbidden memory of Gill feeding her mango in bed rose in her mind. He had trailed the seed over her breasts and then thoroughly removed the sweet, heavenly juices with his tongue. She blinked. 'And…um…sun-baking.'

Gill had the same mango image in his mind and felt his mouth water. He looked at her when she mentioned sun-baking and remembered how she liked to go nude on the beach so her olive skin wasn't marred by white strap marks.

He smiled to himself. Once a hippy, always a hippy. Harriet had been brought up by alternative lifestyle parents who still lived a communal existence in the hinterland of the mid New South Wales coast. They had instilled in her a wonderful sense of justice and fairness and doing unto others, and he knew they had made her the wonderful humanitarian she was today.

And because of this lifestyle he didn't think he'd met anyone quite as at ease with their body or nudity as Harry. At home she barely wore clothes and every opportunity she got to disrobe she took gleefully. And, dear God, what a body it was. As far as he was concerned, she could be permanently naked. But unfortunately…he'd just signed away any rights to seeing her naked ever again.

Her gaze met his and for a moment he felt as if she was thinking the same thing. No more nudity. No more Bondi. No more mangoes or barbeques or *escargots*. At least, not together. Did she feel that loss as keenly as he did or had she had time to get used to it? After all, in their year of separation he had never seriously believed that either of them would make it permanent. But she'd obviously thought about it a lot.

'What are the chances, do you think,' Katya asked in her accented English, 'we will get out of here before any more casualties arrive?'

'Zero,' said Helmut, pessimistic as always.

The turn in conversation brought Gill out of his trance and he reluctantly broke eye contact with Harriet. Their flight left at 7 a.m. tomorrow morning. It wasn't unknown to go twenty-four hours without incoming wounded, but it was the exception rather than the rule.

He found himself in a perverse kind of way hoping there would be. Not that he wished any of the locals ill, he just knew from the last two months that the human carnage was showing no signs of abating, the civil war gathering momentum if anything, and that it was never long between skirmishes. If it was going to happen, just bring it on, he thought. He needed to keep busy today so he didn't have to think about Harriet and the divorce and how badly his life was going to suck without her.

CHAPTER FOUR

1000 HOURS

ON THEIR way to the morning triage meeting, Katya caught up with Harriet.

'One more sleep, Harry,' she said.

Harriet laughed. Katya was the youngest of the three nurses that formed their surgical team and had been with MedSurg Aid Abroad for four years. Harriet loved to listen to her talk. Her grasp of the English language was superb and her accent very easy on the ear, adding a husky quality to what she was saying.

She especially liked it when Katya, the most volatile of the group, lost her cool, which happened from time to time in the presence of such senseless carnage. She would slip back into her native Russian every third or fourth word and especially when she couldn't think of an insulting enough English word.

Katya always said that Russian swear words were much more poetic than English. And listening to her in full flight, Harriet had to admit she was right. It was as if Katya was reciting Tolstoy, the frown on her pretty animated face a reminder that her words weren't really high literature at all.

'You do know how happy we all are that you and Gill are back together.'

Harriet's step faltered briefly. A denial rose to her lips but looking at the joy on her friend's face she didn't have the heart to speak the truth. What was the point? Their mission was over tomorrow. Why not part with everyone thinking she and Gill were going to live happily ever after? This fine group of people wanted so badly for them to be happy, for it to be like it had been. They would all know the truth soon enough.

Harriet smiled and nodded. 'Yes, I do.'

Katya grinned back at her and not for the first time Harriet thought what a good match Gill and Katya would make. In fact, she half suspected that they would have hooked up in her absence. The blonde, petite Russian nurse was very pretty in a perky kind of a way and there had been a time when Katya had first joined their team that she'd had a huge crush on Gill.

Not that Harriet had ever felt threatened by it. If anything, it had been amusing and Katya had been far too young and innocent to take seriously. Gill and the group had been patient and allowed her to get over her hero-worship without an embarrassing confrontation.

But there didn't seem to even be a whiff of anything having happened. No awkwardness between them, no hushed, secretive conversations, no vibe that they knew each other intimately. Just the same friendly banter that had always existed between them. That the whole team thrived on. That gelled them all together.

She'd hoped Gill had found the idea of casual sex during their separation as abhorrent as she had. That their separation had devastated him as much as her. That sex with someone else just didn't rate. But he was a virile man with appetites and she didn't fool herself for a moment that men and women thought the same way about matters relating to sex.

And a year was a long time. A year of living apart, working apart. Harriet had stayed with MedSurg but had joined another surgical team that had gone to different hot-spots and had worked the opposite rotation to Gill's. So when Gill's team had been flying home for a month's R and R, Harriet's team had been flying elsewhere to start their two-month stint.

Communication between them had been complicated by their work assignments. The places they went to and the conditions of the local infrastructure often meant phone or mobile contact was not possible. MedSurg comms centre had enough on their plates, dealing with casualties and air evacuations and managing their ground-level programmes, without being a message centre for idle chit-chat. Only emergency calls for staff were allowed.

Email had been their most efficient communication tool. Separation via electronic mail. Harriet had hated it. She wondered now as they filed into the triage meeting if they would divorce via the internet as well. Would they split up their assets, argue about which books, which CDs belonged to whom?

She imagined her email to him when the decree nisi arrived. *Dear Gill. It's official. We are no longer joined in marriage. You should be receiving the paperwork soon. Have a good life.* Harriet shuddered. She felt so empty thinking about it, but the alternative Gill had suggested this morning made her emptier.

A part-time father who'd rather fly around the world, fixing other people's problems, than be with her and their baby. To have to watch his detachment when he came home and live with him, knowing he had one eye on the calendar. Harriet knew as surely as she knew that she loved him that she'd be more miserable with half of Gill than none of him.

'Oh, great,' muttered Katya beside her as she slipped into the seat next to Harriet. 'Just what I needed on my last day. Casanova.'

Harriet smiled to herself. Sitting opposite them was another reason why Gill and Katya would probably never hook up. Count Benedetto Medici the third. Italian aristocracy, wealthy playboy and MedSurg's newest surgeon. It was standard operating procedure for MSAA to send two full teams to any mission, and unfortunately casualty numbers more than justified it.

The smooth charm of the affluent newbie had well and truly rubbed Katya up the wrong way, her poor-as-dirt background giving her a healthy dislike of men born with silver spoons in their mouths. It was obvious to all but Katya they were hot for each other.

'Morning, Katya,' he said across the table, sending her a smouldering smile.

'Ben,' she said shortly, and Harriet admired her withering dismissal.

She glanced at Gill, who winked at her, and for a second she forgot that they'd be nearly divorced by the time Gill returned to the team next time. The memory of their joining this morning was still fresh in her mind and for a few seconds she remembered how much she loved him and how their romance, too, had blossomed in the diverse melting pot of an MSAA mission.

Gill also remembered. He'd been entering his fourth year with the organisation and had been a little apprehensive about the new RN taking over from Liesel, who was going back to Sweden to get married. It was always a little stressful when someone new joined an already established team.

Would they fit in? Would they complement the existing members, would the fit be seamless or would their presence cause ripples and potentially be disruptive? Would the unity of the team be irreparably damaged? Did they have a sense of humour? Were they willing to fit in with the routines and procedures of the group?

What had been their motivation to join the organisation in the first place? Was it for a genuine humanitarian reason or were they running away from something or dropping out of society? Gill had been around long enough to see the effect one ill-suited person could have on the harmony of a team.

So all these things had been careening through his mind the night he and the rest of the team had met Harriet at a London restaurant, and had been banished in an instant. She had been gorgeous and had fitted in instantly, and they had both known without a single word being spoken that their destinies were entwined.

When they'd left together a couple of hours later there had been no question of saying goodbye at the door. The only question had been which hotel room—his or hers. They'd settled on hers because it had been the closest. And despite knowing that they were heading into the world's latest war zone the next day, they had been up all night.

He remembered how Harriet had been worried the next morning about the consequences. How would the rest of the team feel? Would they judge her? Would they resent her? Should they keep it quiet? So they'd agreed to do that but they'd been so besotted with each other it had been hopeless and they'd given the game away within the first week.

And now here they were, seven years later, weeks away from divorce.

'So,' said Ben. 'Shall we begin?'

Gill reluctantly broke eye contact with his wife. Ex-wife. Better get used to that, he thought. Ex-wife. Ex-wife.

The daily triage meeting was held with as many staff present as possible. Obviously if they were operating it was postponed, but otherwise 10:30 every morning—like clockwork.

Triage was a bit of a misnomer, really. Yes, decisions were made on a case-by-case basis as to which patient got the next available helicopter to a major centre, but it was also a forum to debrief, air problems and talk about more mundane things such as supplies, equipment and procedures.

'Three of my patients stayed in the HDU overnight. The liver lac has priority. His drain losses haven't slowed and I'd like to get him out of here first,' said Ben.

Gill nodded. He had two patients they hadn't been able to evacuate last night and neither would take priority over the liver. One had been lucky and had taken minor shrapnel damage to his gut and the other had a penetrating eye injury that, while serious, was not life-threatening.

These were the decisions they made every day. Who couldn't wait, who had to. Patients triaged in the field as requiring medical or surgical intervention were choppered to the MSAA facility. The objective of the surgical teams was to operate so the immediate threat to the patient's life was alleviated and then evacuate as soon as possible to the most appropriate major centre.

Usually there were a couple of cases that, due to

stretched resources, had to stay behind post-op. In this situation the least critical stayed and were nursed in their limited high-dependency unit. This had five beds and two nurses, with back-up from the surgeons and anaesthetists.

'Comms from HQ this morning has confirmed they can evac everyone,' said Ben.

'Good.' Gill nodded. 'We'll do your liver first then the three abdo traumas then the eye.'

Harriet watched as everyone nodded in agreement. No one batted an eyelid that the patients were recognised by their body parts rather than their names. This had been the hardest thing for her to come to terms with in this field of medicine. Maybe it was the nurse in her but it just didn't seem right to not know a patient's name.

To be fair, a lot of this had to do with the language barrier and the fact that the majority of their patients were in no condition to divulge their names. Seventy-five per cent of their workload were unconscious, and with no IDs their names were impossible to know. But surgeons did have a nasty habit of referring to their patients as a bunch of body parts and it was so dehumanising Harriet knew it was one part of this job she wouldn't miss. But, then, nothing was more dehumanising than war.

'I have an update on yesterday's casualties,' said Theire, the translator, in her soft, heavily accented voice. Now, that was something she would miss. The accents. Every working day she was surrounded by the music of other languages. From the people she worked with to the locals who were unfortunate enough to end up on their operating tables, it was like living in an opera composed by the UN.

She hadn't realised just how deeply it had become a part of her subconscious. Her ears didn't hear it any more but the thought of no longer hearing a mish-mash of foreign tongues was depressing.

Just in this room they had Italian Ben, Russian Katya, German Helmut, Irish Siobhan, Theire, who spoke several of the local dialects, and various English, American and Australian contributions as well. And then there was Gill. He spoke with the careless drawl of a fair dinkum Aussie, but when he spoke French it was like he'd been born there.

She would really miss that. Miss how he would speak French with his parents and grandfather in her presence from time to time, or jokingly ask for an instrument in the language while he was working to crack everyone up, or casually slip into it at home because he knew how much it turned her on. He made love in French, too.

'I have been in contact with the various facilities that our patients were transferred to.' MedSurg always employed a local interpreter for each mission. Their services were invaluable.

'The man with the bullet in his brain did not make it. Nor did the little boy with the traumatic amputation of his leg. The three chest traumas are still in critical conditions but holding their own. The woman with the gut full of shrapnel had to go back for more surgery. They removed an extensive amount of ischaemic large bowel and she now has a colostomy.'

There was silence in the room as they all thought about the people from the day before. Gill had operated on the little boy. The child had lost so much blood, and even as he had been operating to tie off the bleeders and stabilise his condition, he had known deep inside that the child wouldn't make it.

The wound had been incredibly dirty, dragged through

filth and mud as the boy had crawled to safety. It was always going to be a matter of whether his profoundly hypovolaemic state or a massive bacterial infection would kill him first. Gill wanted to punch the table at the unfairness of it all. What had a child of eight done to deserve that?

He looked at Harriet and could see she was affected by the news as well. He suddenly envied her turning her back on all of this. To never have to look into the eyes of another man, woman or child injured through the stupidity of war. For the first time he wondered how long he could do it for. There was always going to be another war. Could he do this for ever? He'd always thought he would but…

She gave him a sympathetic smile and he shook himself out of his reverie. Their divorce conversation had obviously got to him. He just needed a break. Two months of this kind of stuff was tough mentally. But this was what he did. This was who he was.

CHAPTER FIVE

'GILL, can you review your abdo trauma from last night? He's febrile and tachycardic. His drain losses are increasing as well.'

Damn it! He must have missed something. He'd spent two hours picking shrapnel out of the rebel soldier's intestines and was confident that they'd removed it all. But as thorough as he'd been, Gill knew that the chances of missing a little hole somewhere, caused by the trajectory of the shrapnel, was always a possibility.

'I'll be right there,' he said, smiling at the HDU nurse.

Harriet rolled her eyes as Megan turned a pretty shade of pink and beamed back at the sexy surgeon. *Her* husband. For another few weeks anyway. Man, he should be banned from smiling. She couldn't blame Megan for feeling a little flushed, it made *her* go positively weak at the knees.

She watched them as they walked side by side and then disappeared into the room that housed the HDU. How was it possible to make a set of plain blue baggy scrubs sexy? She remembered how she had thought him breathtakingly gorgeous that night in London dressed to impress and later how magnificent he was undressed, but equally impressive was how he filled out a set of scrubs.

It was like the minute he donned them he became Dr Guillaume Remy, surgeon. The sense of authority that exuded from him was powerful, virile—almost sexual. The blue theatre cap tied and anchored at the back of his neck just below his hairline made him look even sexier.

If anyone were to ask her in years to come what her fondest memory was of their time together, there would be no hesitation. Seeing Gill in his scrubs and cap, laughing his deep, sexy laugh, oblivious to his innate sex appeal. Harriet felt a moment of panic as she stored away the memory. One more day of memories and that was it.

Gill took one look at his patient and knew he was going to have to reopen him. The man was burning up and muttered unintelligibly, the words both foreign and muffled by the face mask. Megan gave Gill the hand-held ultrasound and he could feel the rigidity of the man's abdomen as the transducer glided through the gel. There was a significant amount of free fluid visible.

'I'll mobilise the team,' he said to Megan.

Gill strode down the corridors, figuring everyone would have adjourned back to the dining area for another cup of artificial stimulant.

Only Harriet and Siobhan were there. 'Let's go,' he said. 'We have to reopen the soldier.'

The soldier. Harriet shook her head as she stood. He'd looked no more than sixteen and had refused to give Theire his name. What was wrong with the world? Babies fighting wars?

But that's what they did. This was the organisation's

mission. It didn't matter how young or old, male or female, civilian or military, goodie or baddie. If you were injured and needed surgery, the doors were always open. There were no moral or ethical judgments—it was just patch 'em up and ship 'em out.

'I'll alert the others,' said Harriet.

'Where's Theire?' he asked.

'Making some more calls,' replied Siobhan as they moved past him to go and set up the theatre.

'I'll get her to talk to the patient. I'll also see Ben about evac-ing him out with the liver. See you there in five,' Gill said.

Harriet and Siobhan located the team in all their scattered locations, which wasn't difficult, given their close confines. There wasn't the infrastructure for a paging system so word of mouth was how it usually worked, except when there were mass casualties arriving. Then a hand-operated siren was used by Dr Kelly Prentice, the on-site medical director, who took the call from comms. It wailed mournfully between the two buildings occupied by MedSurg, spreading its bad news like an involuntary shudder to the furthest reaches of the complex.

MedSurg had set up in an old whitewashed convent that harked back a couple of hundred years to colonial times. Kelly used this building for the medical side of the mission and across the dirt a long, rickety concrete path connected it to the old orphanage building, which was where the surgical side was housed. Gill's territory.

The area had once been a thriving community—now it was just a few buildings in the middle of nowhere on the periphery of a war zone. The buildings had been used until the recent civil unrest as a medical facility. The nearest towns were at least one hundred kilometres in any direction, the nearest hospital at least two hundred and fifty kilometres away.

The old orphanage now used as the surgical block was a double-storey building with wide, open verandahs that wrapped around the entire building to take advantage of any breeze that might be wafting by. Two downstairs rooms had been converted to operating theatres with basic tables, anaesthetic machines, monitors and overhead lights, and smaller side rooms each housed ancient instrument sterilisers and served as storage rooms.

Another of the bigger rooms was set up as the HDU/recovery area and there were various smaller rooms used for their triage meetings and as a communal kitchen and lounge area.

Upstairs were the living quarters, which, although were small, had French-style doors that opened onto the verandahs. Not that it was actually that safe to be sitting out there a lot of the time, but the tantalising luxury was there if anyone had the nerve.

By the time the rest of the team arrived, Harriet and Siobhan had everything under control. Siobhan was scrubbing up when Gill strode into the theatre. 'Everything good to go?' he asked a masked Harriet.

Gill forgot the urgency for a fleeting moment. Harriet in her mask, her features completely hidden from his gaze, was mystically beautiful. The deep brown depths of her eyes were emphasised tenfold, and he felt like he was falling into a warmed vat of deep rich chocolate and drowning.

Her luxurious hair was also hidden within the confines of the most unglamorous headwear on the planet, but he still couldn't disguise his fascination with it. He knew that beneath the almost see-through blue fabric it was up in a ponytail and, despite her complaints about hat hair when she removed it between cases, it always made him forget to breathe.

'Yup.' Harriet nodded briskly and busied herself with opening the sterile packs, ignoring the brooding presence of her husband. She daren't look at him. She could feel the intensity of his gaze like he had X-ray vision. What was he thinking? Was he reconsidering his position? Or just trying to visualise her naked? Suddenly the mask felt claustrophobic and she was grateful when he left.

Siobhan entered a few moments later, her arms held slightly aloft and bent at the elbow, water dripping from them occasionally. She picked up the sterile towel that sat folded on top of the sterile gown that Harriet had opened for her and placed on a stainless-steel trolley.

Siobhan dried her hands and arms thoroughly on the cloth and then picked up the gown, climbing into it with an efficient sterile technique and turning so Harriet could tie it at the neck. Next she moved to the size-six gloves Harriet had also opened and in a couple of smooth movements had gloved up. Siobhan set about sorting out the tray of instruments on her sterile draped table and she and Harriet conducted a count of the swabs, towels and instruments most likely to be used during the procedure. Harriet scribbled the numbers on the count sheet so they knew how many extra bits and pieces had to be kept track of.

Then Gill entered the room in the same fashion as Siobhan and after he'd dried his hands he gowned, and Harriet had to get up close to tie his gown for him. She lingered for a moment too long and could tell by the stiffness of his shoulders that he was more than aware of it. He smelt so good and it was hard to believe she would never see him operate again after today.

The patient came in then, accompanied by Katya and Joan, and it was all hands on deck. Joan and Helmut anaesthetised him and Katya left to scrub in as well. Harriet was the circulating nurse—euphemism for gopher. Anything any of the sterile people needed, she fetched. The three nurses took it in turns, rotating from scrubbing to circulating, and the system worked well.

Finally everything was ready. The suction was working, the diathermy was in order and an earthing plate had been stuck to the patient's thigh. The patient was draped and the surgical area prepped with Betadine. Joan signalled she was happy with their patient's condition and for Gill to commence.

As he removed the staples he had placed less than twelve hours ago, Harriet placed an Ella Fitzgerald CD in the portable player and switched it to background. It was Gill's favourite, his grandfather's influence, and he loved to listen to her dulcet tones as he operated. She knew it helped him relax into the job at hand and, well, she'd suffered worse surgeons' tastes in her many years as an operating nurse.

One particular surgeon she had worked for had insisted on listening to arcane, obscure Gregorian chants, and by the time the theatre list had ended, she'd always been at screaming point.

Gill quickly opened the abdominal wound. 'Retractor,' he said, and Siobhan placed it in his hand. He inserted the heavy metal contraption into the wound and turned the cogs, watching as it slowly cranked open, taking the skin and layers of adipose tissue with it, pushing them back to either side to give a clear view of the abdominal cavity.

'OK, folks,' he said, 'let's find us a hole.'

Gill knew this could take five minutes or two hours. Finding a little tear was sometimes like trying to find a needle in a haystack. He decided to try a short-cut first.

'Saline.'

Gill tipped the sterile bowl full of warmed sterile saline gently into the abdominal cavity, submerging the bowel, and waited. After a minute a small bubble squirmed to the surface and popped. As he'd suspected, he'd missed something. Now he just had to find it! And hope that one bubble meant only one hole!

It was probably on a posterior side somewhere. He'd have to start from the top and work his way down. Siobhan used a sucker to remove the fluid and Gill began the painstaking process of checking every centimetre of the intestine. It felt warm in his gloved hands and sort of rippled. It was all gooey and squishy, like a bowl of warm jelly, but looked and felt like a string of sausages.

He heard Harriet humming to 'Cry me a River' and glanced up. She always did that. Even scrubbed, she would hum along to Ella, completely unaware she was doing it. He'd missed that this last year, watching Harriet move around a theatre, humming quietly to herself. Or standing next to him, rubbing shoulders, passing him instruments as she hummed away. He'd had it back for a blissful two months and she was going to snatch it all away again.

His eyes flicked back to what he was doing. He really needed to concentrate, damn it! He was too aware of her. Today in particular. Today, the day he'd signed pieces of paper that would put them asunder for ever—it was most distracting! He was excruciatingly aware of her every move

around the theatre. Opening things, writing things, murmuring something to Helmut and humming along to Ella.

'Could you adjust the light, Harry?' he asked. Why, he
didn't know. The light position was just fine. But then she
moved closer and reached up so the fabric of her scrubs
pulled taut across her chest and he could smell her
perfume, and he was very glad he had asked.

She'd moved it a millimetre when he said, 'That's fine.'

Harriet glanced at him, a puzzled look in her eyes—
she'd barely moved the wretched thing! Only his eyes were
visible to her gaze and she raised her eyebrows at him.
Their gazes locked and she saw a flicker of desire brighten
the grey. She rolled her eyes at him and stepped back.

After another twenty minutes of looking, he finally
located a small nick on the posterior wall of the ascend-
ing colon not far from the appendix.

'Bingo,' he murmured. 'Suture.'

Gill over sewed the minor tear, and then gave the entire
area a good lavage with warmed saline to wash out any
debris that might have found its way into the abdominal
cavity through the small hole. Fortunately the patient
already had triple antibiotics on board to cover infection.
Siobhan suctioned the saline out again as Gill reinserted a
new drain through the old tract.

Harriet and Siobhan finished their final count and were
satisfied they had everything back that they'd started with.
Gill went ahead and closed the abdomen. She watched, fascinated, as she always did. His fingers were quick but
careful and watching him sew up was like watching
someone experienced at embroidering or needlepoint. It
was a true skill and he was a master.

The phone rang. 'Theatre. Harriet speaking.'

'Good morning. This is Genevieve from MSAA communications centre. We have an urgent message for Dr Remy. Is he around?'

Harriet clutched the phone, a sixth sense making her uneasy. It had to be bad for comms to be passing on a message. 'He's closing an abdomen at the moment. I'm his wife—you can leave it with me.'

Thank God for the mask! Harriet could feel herself blush as Gill looked up abruptly from his work. It was a bit rich, making a claim on a marriage that she had in effect just ended. His eyes held a slightly mocking expression.

'Who is it?' he asked.

'Comms. Urgent message for you.'

'Tell them to give it to…my wife.'

Harriet didn't miss the derision, although she was sure the others hadn't picked up on it. 'Did you hear that?' Harriet asked Genevieve.

'Yes. OK. We have a phone call from his father. Henri Remy has had a massive heart attack and is in a critical but stable condition in Coronary Care.'

Harriet closed her eyes briefly and swallowed hard. No. Not Henri. Gill was exceptionally close to his grandfather. Hell, so was she. It was hard to believe that a man who had a heart the size of Henri's would ever succumb to human frailties. Decorated by his country for showing extreme bravery in the face of the enemy in occupied France during the war, he was Gill's hero. The news would hit him hard.

'What?' Gill asked as he watched Harriet slowly replace the receiver and look at him with anguish in her eyes. His hand, complete with stitch holder, was poised above the partially closed abdomen.

'It's Henri,' she said, pronouncing it with the correct French inflection.

'Is he dead?' he asked bluntly.

Harriet flinched at Gill's directness but noticed his vice-like grip on the instrument in his hand and wanted to go to him. Scrubbed or not. Sterile or not. 'No.' She shook her head and tried to expel the tremor from her voice. 'MI. He's critical.'

Their gazes locked again and they shared a brief moment of solidarity. She saw the disbelief and shock and watched as he blinked rapidly a few times.

Gill nodded and held Harriet's gaze a bit longer. Then he gave himself a mental shake and closed the wound.

CHAPTER SIX

HARRIET sat opposite Gill in the lounge. He had pulled his hat off and was running a hand back and forth through his rumpled hair as he had an animated discussion in French with his father. He was sitting on the edge of the chair, bent forward at the waist, his elbows on his knees, his head bowed.

She was sitting in a similar fashion, their knees almost touching. She fought a battle and lost over touching him. The sensible side of her, which was trying to step back, resisted, but the emotional side caved in. He was still her husband and even if he wasn't, which was soon to be the case, he was a significant part of her life and he had just received bad news. The urge to comfort him was strong. As she would have wanted to comfort anyone in this situation.

She placed her hand on his knee and he glanced at her as he continued his conversation, giving her a grim smile. He stopped worrying his hair and covered her hand with his. He stroked her fingers and then curled his into hers, linking them together.

Gill replaced the phone and they both sat there quietly

for a few minutes, Gill still holding her hand, his thumb caressing back and forth across her knuckles.

'They're very worried about him,' he said finally. 'He's arrested twice and keeps having runs of VT.'

'Oh, Gill, I'm so sorry,' she whispered. He looked awful. She'd never seen him look his age before, but right at this moment he looked every one of his forty years. His forehead was creased with concern and he looked pale and haggard, like he'd been operating for twenty-four hours straight.

'He's eighty-eight. I guess we keep forgetting that. He's always been so larger than life.'

She nodded because suddenly she felt too emotional to speak. She could feel tears pricking at her eyes as she imagined Henri, big, strong Henri, lying helpless in a hospital bed.

Gill looked at her and saw the tears shining in her eyes. He wanted to say, Hey come on, he'll be OK—but he couldn't when he wasn't sure if his grandfather would pull through this at all. Things didn't look good.

'Harry,' he said, his voice conveying what he couldn't say. He felt kind of lost and he so wanted to feel her in his arms, lean on her a little. Seek a little comfort in a place that he knew better and liked better than almost anywhere. He held out his arms and sighed gratefully when she didn't argue or hesitate. Just fell to the floor, pushing herself between his legs, and hugged him for all she was worth.

It felt so good, being like this. Everything seemed right with the world from this perspective. It didn't matter that outside these walls a stupid civil war raged or that his grandfather was probably going to die. Harriet obliterated it all. Wrapped up in her embrace, everything was OK.

But the embrace couldn't last for ever and Harriet let

him go. She sat back on her haunches, his knees level with her shoulders. He looked down into her delectable face, etched with worry.

'At least it happened today,' she said, searching for something positive. She knew that Gill, despite his deep affection and loyalty towards his grandfather, would have been very uncomfortable leaving them mid-mission. It was part of that humanitarian streak and work ethic his grandfather had instilled in him. 'Everything is already arranged for your departure tomorrow. Or are you leaving immediately?'

'No. There's only today to get through. I may as well see the mission out. It probably couldn't be arranged much before tomorrow anyway.'

Harriet swallowed before she said what she was about to say. It was a possibility she didn't want to think about but it had to be said. 'What if he…?'

'Dies before I get home?' He watched as Harriet nodded miserably. She said what he'd been thinking, but he knew it hadn't been an easy thing for her to raise.

'By the sound of it, that's a distinct possibility. But given how far from home we are there's not much I can do about that.'

They both reflected for a few moments on the gloomy statement. Of course, Henri was going to die eventually. He was an old man but the vitality of the Remy patriarch had lulled them all into a false sense of security.

Harriet absently ran her hands along Gill's thighs. She'd barely seen him for a year but two months back in his life and his bed and she'd slipped easily into old intimacies. What was the expression—old habits died hard?

'Do you remember the first time I met Henri?' she asked.

Gill heard the husky quality of her voice and it grabbed his heart strings and pulled tight. He smiled at the memory. 'Of course. You were an instant hit.'

He had said to her, 'Today is your lucky day. Not only are you with my handsome grandson but I am cooking for you a French delicacy—*escargots*!'

'Oh, goody,' she'd said, and had clapped her hands. 'I've always wanted to try snails.'

'It was Grandfather's litmus paper for relationships. Well…my relationships anyway. You were the only girl who didn't screw up her nose at the thought of snails.'

'Silly girls,' she said, trying to lighten the atmosphere. 'The way he cooks them in that delicate creamy sauce, man, they're good. Actually, I was just relived he hadn't said frogs' legs.'

Gill laughed, and it felt good to talk about happier times. 'Do you know what he said to me that afternoon, before we left?'

Harriet smiled and shook her head. 'No. What?'

'He said, "Guillaume, if you don't marry that girl, I will."'

Harriet laughed, and Gill joined her. She saw the worry ease a little and she was grateful that she could take his mind off it a little. Actually, marrying Gill had been almost like being married to Henri. They were very alike, and Harriet only had to look into Henri's face, lined with wisdom and experience, to know how Gill was going to age.

Gracefully. With a full head of distinguished grey hair and a lasting firmness and tone to his body that belied his age. Gill's smile would get saucier and his wit even sharper. And he would still speak French to her and she would still swoon. And he would cook her the most magnificent *escargots* to his grandfather's secret family recipe.

She shook herself. No. Not her. Someone else would have that right. She didn't doubt he would be snapped up in a hurry. He was a great catch…as long as a baby wasn't on the agenda. And that was fine. He deserved to find happiness again. She wished it for him, she really did. Just as she wished it for herself. Just as she knew that only a baby would make her truly happy again.

His thumb found her wedding ring and he rubbed it back and forth as he stared at it on her slim finger. It had been his grandmother's. 'You're still wearing it,' he said.

'I'm still married.' She shrugged. One year ago she'd separated from him but physical separation was much easier than mental separation. Things like wedding rings and giving up Remy as her name and missing his toiletries next to hers in the bathroom cabinet were much harder to come to terms with.

'You still wear yours,' she murmured, fondling the wide gold band she had given to him on their wedding day. She remembered how she used to make him take his off and she would take off hers and she could slip hers inside the circumference of his. It had been like a confirmation that she would always be snug and safe and supported in his love.

'We're not divorced yet.'

She looked into his grey eyes and felt a weird kinship. They had always thought so much alike. 'I guess I'll have to give it back,' she said wistfully, looking down at the narrow band.

The ring and all it represented—not just Gill's love but its heritage and family value—were so integral to her that parting with it would be gut-wrenching. She may have only had it for six years but the ring that Henri had worn on his little finger for the last thirty years, after his dear Renée's death, had tremendous sentimental value.

Henri had taken her aside after their engagement and told her it would honour him if she were to take Renée's ring as her wedding band, and she had been touched and worn it with love and pride. That it had history and meaning, not just for Gill and her but for past lovers, had always made it extra-special for Harriet.

'No,' he said quietly, still fingering the thin metal. 'Henri would want you to keep it.'

'I couldn't,' she gasped, pulling her hand off his thigh and sitting back on her heels. 'It's a family heirloom.'

'Henri gave it to you because he loves you and thinks you're worthy of my grandmother's ring. Whether you're married to me or not, that won't change.'

It seemed strange to be talking about Henri as an active, vital person when on the other side of the world he was fighting for his very life. The mood changed to sombre again, the talk of parting ways not helping.

'Is your father going to keep you up to date?'

'Yes. He's going to ring again in a few hours.'

'Make sure you send them my love. Tell them I'm thinking of them and to kiss Henri for me.'

'Why don't you do it yourself? Come back with me tomorrow. Don't fly to London first. I'll get a direct flight home from the capital. Come back with me. Henri would love to see you again.'

MedSurg, being an English charitable organisation, was based in the UK and had its headquarters in London. It was usual to fly teams out of wherever they might be at the end of a mission into London for a few days' R and R and then fly them back to their homes. It made up for the lousy pay.

'Gill…' She couldn't. It was just too hard. The strings had to be cut and the longer she kept them tied, no matter the reason, the harder it would be.

'You know the irony of this is I was going to ask you to spend a few days with me in London…to try and sort things out…reconnect. I guess it's too late…'

'About two years too late. I can't come back to Australia with you. It's too hard, Gill. We both know where we stand. I want a baby. You don't. We're at an impasse. I will go and see Henri if…' She didn't want to say the obvious. 'When I get back in a few days. I've always kept in close touch with your family, you must know that. Don't make this harder than it is.'

She wanted to say if only he'd agree to a baby, but she knew he'd say if only she'd stuck to their original plan. They'd been down this road too many times before and with Henri's fate weighing heavily on their minds she didn't want to travel back over the same territory. Their energies would be better spent thinking positive thoughts for a swift recovery.

CHAPTER SEVEN

1300 HOURS

THE two surgical teams left the building together and walked across to the medical building. Once a week, providing they weren't in the middle of surgery, the surgical and medical teams joined together and ran an immunisation clinic.

Most of the countries MedSurg serviced had very low levels of childhood immunisation. Part of MSAA's directive was mass vaccination, and they employed people in the field, working in partnership with the World Health Organisation to co-ordinate local vaccination programmes.

Yellow fever, a potentially fatal mosquito-borne illness, was prevalent in this particular area, and the teams had been tasked to immunise as many locals as was possible during their stay. Thanks to the field operatives, come clinic days there were usually hundreds, if not thousands of men, women and children lining up for their shots. They mostly came in MSAA trucks, but a lot of locals just walked in from nearby villages.

Therefore it was all hands on deck. Some of the surgical teams grumbled about it but Harriet quite liked it. It got them out amongst the locals, instead of staying cloistered inside the same sets of walls for two months. They could become very insulated inside and it was nice to think they were doing something proactive for once, instead of reactive.

The idea of public health had always been attractive to Harriet, and as she walked in the heat she thought it could be an area of nursing she could get involved with now she was leaving MedSurg. She looked at Gill's back as she walked behind him and thought how much leaving the organisation didn't seem to matter any more. A few years ago it would have been unthinkable.

But so much had happened in a couple of years and she'd done a lot of soul-searching. Yes, she loved her work, enjoyed being a theatre nurse, but if she was totally honest, Gill had been the reason she'd stuck with it for so long. She never liked reducing her patients to body parts, as so often happened in the surgical setting, and public health would actually allow some sort of rapport and relationship to develop between her and her patients.

Several tents had been set up outside the medical building under the shade of the few remaining trees that existed in the dust bowl that surrounded them. They were big and looked as old as the buildings themselves, and were obviously very hardy to have survived all this time when other greenery had long ago succumbed to the arid heat.

The clinic was just getting under way as the team arrived.

'So pleased you could join us,' said Dr Kelly Prentice in her brisk New York twang, grinning eagerly at her recruits as she swatted away the ever-present flies. 'Pull up a pew. You know the routine.'

Out of habit Harriet sat down next to Gill and then spent a moment dithering about whether she should have or not. Helmut sat on the other side of her and he smiled at her as he said, 'Bet I can do more than you.'

Harriet smiled back at him and forgot her dithering. 'This isn't a race, Helmut.' She rolled her eyes at him. 'Competitive men!' He laughed and started jabbing his first customer.

Between each chair was a small table with a supply of the vaccine and a box of gloves, and on the other side a sharps bin. Harriet smiled at her first patient and started work.

Gill looked up from his work at the teeming mass of humanity waiting patiently in line. An array of colourful fabrics dazzled the eye and Gill marvelled with all that they'd been through, their pride in their culture still remained strong. The crowd was as big as usual, about six or seven hundred at a guess, but he knew from past experience that with twenty health-care professionals administering the vaccine, it'd be all over in an hour.

He tried to concentrate on his work. But with thinking of his grandfather and with Harriet in his peripheral vision, talking and trying to make the children laugh as she worked, he was failing badly. She was a natural with the kids and had their shy, serious expressions erased in a flash, replaced with big white grins.

He had heard Helmut's challenge and knew he would win hands down. Being fast wasn't Harriet's style. It wasn't that she wasn't efficient, she just thrived on making a connection, taking some time to make her patients feel like individuals.

She looked up at him and caught him staring. He smiled at her and she smiled back as she flapped at some flies. She was glowing, in her element, despite the heat and the flies, as she turned back to a little girl who was shyly showing her a raggedy old toy that had seen better days.

Gill continued to work through his line, smiling at every patient, wondering what the hell must be going through their heads. The things these people had lived through and seen. They took their needles stoically, even the children. What was one tiny needle compared with a horrific civil war? Compared to having no food in your belly or your house burnt to the ground or your parents killed? Compared to dying from yellow fever, as so many of their countrymen had?

No. There were no hysterics here. No cajoling kids and bribing them with ice creams and sweets, like back at home. Just a resigned silence, a calm acceptance. Someone down the line, a woman, began to sing a tribal tune and others joined in, and suddenly the lines were swaying to the rhythm. It was like listening to ancient music being sung by a gospel choir in a foreign tongue.

Gill marvelled at the people's resilience. They were standing in the dirt, their feet bare, the sun beating down relentlessly, in a place torn apart by war, and yet they could still sing. They could still rejoice.

He smiled at a beaming Harriet who was also getting into the groove. There was something indomitable about these people, defiant as they raised their voices in pride. They seemed to be saying, This is our home and we will survive.

Gill felt a sudden pang hit him in the chest and ripple outwards. What was it? Maybe it was his grandfather, maybe it was saying goodbye to Harriet, maybe there was magic in this music, but listening to their tribal tempo, which seemed to be coming from the very earth beneath their feet, he had a strong urge to go home. To ground himself.

He turned to look at Harriet as he absently brushed some flies from his face and he felt the ripples intensify.

She sat on her chair in her scrubs, talking to a mother while she nursed a baby on her lap. The babe had its head snuggled into Harriet's breasts and tiny fingers wrapped around Harriet's slender index finger.

The two women couldn't possibly understand each other but there was something universal about babies that crossed language barriers and cultures. Harriet looked radiant and for the first time ever he imagined how it would be to have her holding their baby on her lap. His baby. Watching her belly blossom and then nurturing their baby at her breast.

A small noise in front of him brought him back to the task at hand. A little boy was looking at him apprehensively with big round eyes. He looked from Gill to the needle he'd been holding poised in the air for too long now and then back at Gill again.

'It's OK, little mate,' he said, and ruffled the boy's hair, giving him a reassuring smile. The boy looked dubious but he took his vaccination without a whimper.

Gill made a concerted effort to control his scattered thoughts. It was hot and his grandfather was critically ill. And it was his last day here. He was always a little stir-crazy after being away from home for two months.

So, she was nursing a cute baby. Babies were cute, that's how they sucked you in. It wasn't until 2 a.m. feeds, no sex for six months and eating cornflakes for tea that you realised you'd been conned.

He liked his life. So had she. He liked dining out most nights, going to the movies, the ballet and the theatre. And making love till 2 a.m. And he most definitely liked his cornflakes for breakfast. Actually, not even then. Eggs Benedict was a much better breakfast at a dinky little sidewalk café.

Damn it all—they'd talked about this. She had agreed. After one scare and years of dating women who sooner or later had wanted his babies, he'd been ecstatic to find one who didn't. She'd changed the rules. Not him. And, he thought as he jabbed yet another child, what about the population problem of the world? How often had they discussed that and decided they didn't want to contribute?

Why, Harry, why? He jabbed another child. I would have given you anything you wanted, anything. But you want this? You want the one thing that I don't. The one thing that gives me hives just thinking about it.

He noticed a big purulent sore on the arm of the next child that the flies were enjoying immensely, and it finally made him put a lid on his rising frustration. He jabbed the boy in the opposite arm and with Theire's help explained to the mother to go up to the medical facility and get it looked at.

These clinics were a good opportunity to treat any and all ailments of the local population, and he'd already sent several patients over to the medical building, suffering from various superficial skin and eye conditions rampant in such a tropical environment. He'd even sent a man across who, he suspected, might have tuberculosis.

The crowd was at last thinning when he heard a most awful noise. He felt like a hand had rammed into his intestines and was squeezing really hard. It was a sound of deep distress and it was coming from Harriet.

He turned to her quickly in time to see her saying, 'Gill!'

She was holding an infant who looked very close to death, flies buzzing around the child's face like vultures circling road kill. The anguish on her face said it all. Please, help! Do something.

'Theire,' he yelled, keeping his eyes on the child, gently

examining the scrap of skin and bones. He looked at the mother and the look of utter human misery and despair there was gut-wrenching. He'd seen that look so often in this war, and other wars all round the world, but it never got any easier to witness.

She was trembling all over and had her hands clasped together like she was praying. Bargaining with God. She was making a low keening noise in the back of her throat as if that's all she was capable of, as if grief had stricken her mute. She knows, thought Gill. She knows her child is going to die.

'Oh, Gill, it's too late. The fever's too advanced,' cried Harriet, her voice etched with pain.

Gill knew she was right. The child's skin had a yellowy-green tinge and the whites of his big brown eyes were also yellowed. Jaundice. The symptom that gave yellow fever its name. He was in liver failure.

He watched as Harriet flapped a hand back in forth in front of the little one's face, swatting away the stubborn little black flies that had zeroed in on the exudate from his eyes and the dried blood at the corners of his mouth. She was making growling noises at them, frustrated at their persistence.

He glanced back at the mother, who was looking down at her child, her face cloaked in grief. She looked utterly destroyed, and Gill tried to imagine how he would feel in her position. Not just that his baby was dying but that he hadn't been able to protect and keep his family safe as he was supposed to. He never wanted to be in her position.

'Ask her how long her child has been like this,' said Gill to Theire as she arrived on the scene.

There was an exchange during which Gill continued to examine the child.

'She says he had a fever and vomiting about a week ago and then got better. He's been yellow for a couple of days. She has walked for two days to bring him here. He won't eat or drink.'

The child could barely hold his head up and keep his eyes open. He was practically unconscious. His fontanelle was very sunken, as were his eyes, and his lips and the mucous membranes of his mouth were cracked and bleeding.

'When did he last pass urine?' asked Gill.

There was another brief exchange. 'Not for over a day now.'

Renal failure as well. 'How old is he?'

Theire repeated the question to the distraught mother. 'Six months,' she relayed back.

'Why did she wait, Gill?' asked a distressed Harriet. 'She waited at the end of the line. She should have brought him straight up.'

Gill gave her hand a squeeze. They both knew that it probably wouldn't have made much difference. 'Because that's what these poor people do, Harriet, they wait.'

'His name, Theire? What's his name?' she asked, turning to the interpreter, blinking back hot tears.

'Nimuk.'

'Stay here and finish up,' said Gill, standing. 'We're nearly done. I'll take him in to Kelly.'

'Nimuk,' she said, handing the child over. 'His name is Nimuk.'

Her eyes burned with a fierce light, boring into his. Gill nodded as he scooped the dying baby from his wife's arms. 'Come on, Nimuk,' Gill crooned, as much for Harriet as for the poor baby.

She watched as he strode quickly to the medical

building. He looked so tall and capable, the baby looking even smaller, more fragile than it was, pressed against his broad chest. Theire followed slowly, allowing the mother to use her as a crutch. Her painfully thin legs, legs that had trekked for two days, suddenly seemed boneless and not able to support her meagre weight. She was too shocked to even walk.

Gill disappeared inside and Harriet knew that she had seen the last of Nimuk. A tear slid down her cheek. She wiped it away, turned back, smiled at her next patient and jabbed.

CHAPTER EIGHT

1400 HOURS

LUNCH was a sombre affair. Gill joined them just as they were sitting down to sandwiches and airline fruit juice. Harriet sought his face, searching it for something positive.

He shook his head. 'He's still hanging on. Kelly got an IV in but it's palliative only.'

'What about choppering him out?' Harriet asked.

There was silence in the room as everyone looked at their plates and tried to pretend they weren't there. They had all seen Nimuk and known how futile any intervention would be. They also understood that some patients just got to you. They clouded your judgment.

'He's in multi-organ failure. He has acidosis not compatible with life. His lactate is through the roof,' Gill said gently, moving to sit down beside her. He stroked a finger down her cheek and cupped her face. 'It's too late, Harry.'

Harriet swallowed the lump that had lodged in her throat and squeezed her eyes shut as she nodded her head. 'I know,' she said, her voice husky with emotion. 'I'm sorry… I know.'

The gentle caress of his thumb on her face was

heavenly but was shredding her emotional fortitude. She placed her hand over his and gently pulled it away. 'Thank you,' she mouthed.

She cleared her throat and waved her hand dismissively. 'Sorry, guys, ignore me. I've always been too emotional.' And she picked up her sandwich.

'This is true,' said Helmut.

And everyone laughed, including Harriet. With the mood lightened a little, lunch proceeded. There was general conversation about what everyone was going to do in London and how they were going to spend their two months off.

'Have you heard any more about your grandfather?' Siobhan asked Gil.

'No. If I don't hear anything in the next couple of hours, I'll ring my father,' said Gill.

There was a return to a more sombre mood again until Joan spoke up. 'Come on, guys. Best and worst. It's our last day. We always play it on our last day.'

'Best and worst?' asked Benedetto, who was the only one remaining at the table from the other surgical team, much to Katya's chagrin.

'It's a game our team plays at the end of a mission,' said Katya, her voice leaving him in no doubt that he wasn't welcome to join in.

Gill laughed. 'Don't mind Katya. She has no manners. Of course you must join us. In fact, you should go first. You have to tell us what's been the best part of the mission for you and the worst.'

Ben smiled. 'Hah! That is easy. Katya. Dear, sweet Katya with the beautiful face and the shrewish tongue. She has been the best and worst of my time here.'

People laughed and Katya blushed.

'I shall miss her when I go back to my home on the Amalfi coast...unless she wishes to join me for a little holiday in Positano?'

'I would rather drink bad vodka.'

There was more general laughter and they moved on. 'My best has been having Harry back,' said Joan, and there was a general murmur of agreement.

'Why, thank you, kind lady,' said Harriet with a smile, and then remembered that this would be the last time she would see these people, work with them, and the smile left her eyes.

'Worst... Hmm, let me see. The food?'

'Oh, hell, yes,' groaned Helmut, as he ripped the lid off his second juice tub. 'I'd kill for a beer. A nice cold German beer. That's my worst—no beer. And my best, well, Harry, of course, but also that pneumonectomy we did right at the beginning. That was a fine piece of work, Guillaume.'

There were more murmurs of agreement. Gill had been really happy with it, too. The lung had been a mess, having taken a chunk of flying metal. The fact that the man had survived at all was a miracle. Gill had had little choice but to completely remove the lung.

Had he had time and been in a major centre with every machine that went ping and the back-up of thoracic surgeons, he could have attempted to save some of it, but that wasn't what field medicine was about. The objective of this kind of surgery was to stabilise the patient for transfer to a more major facility.

They operated with basic equipment, the bare minimum. It was fix and fly. Not try something and see if it worked. There was no time for risky or fancy. No time for lengthy repair procedures. Fix and fly. Fix and fly.

'My best is definitely having the whole team back together,' said Siobhan, grinning at Harriet, 'and I think I'll have to agree with Helmut about the worst. What I wouldn't give for a nice pint of Dublin Guinness.'

Helmut made gagging noises. Helmut was not a Guinness fan. 'I would rather drink bad vodka, too,' he said, and laughter broke out again.

It was Katya's turn. *'Da,'* she said. 'Having Harriet back has been the best. The very best.'

'OK, stop now, you guys, you're embarrassing me!' said Harriet. And making her feel equally rotten. She knew that the expectation in the room was that she'd be returning. And she knew she wasn't.

'My worst?' She glared across the table at Ben and Harriet laughed. Poor Ben. He feigned a wounded expression but Harriet could tell he revelled in her attention. 'The bloody flies,' she said, still looking directly at Ben. 'Buzz, buzz, buzzing around. Always buzzing.'

Ben roared with laughter. 'You are the only person who has ever compared me to a fly.'

'Welcome to the real world, Count,' she said, her face deadly serious.

'OK, OK,' Gill interrupted. 'My turn.' He felt Harriet tense beside him. 'Well, let's see, it'd look pretty bad if I didn't say Harry as well but, then…' He grinned. 'That pneumonectomy was good.' In fact, having Harry back with the team had been indescribably joyous, but he knew the ending and it was anything but.

'Way to go, fool,' said Katya in her usual blunt fashion. 'Chose a lung over your woman. When she leaves you again, don't say I didn't warn you.'

Harriet knew Katya was only joking but the reality of

the situation hit and she felt a wave of regret wash over her and lowered her eyes for a moment. She was leaving. And this time she wouldn't be coming back.

'Worst…well, there have been a few of them just today. The news of my grandfather was pretty bad, so was Nimuk.' And then there were the papers that he had signed that morning. He looked at Harriet and noted the tense line of her body. Did she think he was going to air that here?

'And I get the whole beer thing, too, but I think my very worst is breaking up.' He heard Harriet's swift intake of breath and met her eyes as she gave him a searching look. 'Breaking up is hard to do,' he said, looking at Harriet intently. Then, remembering the rest of the group, he returned his gaze to them. 'It's good to have a break and go home but I'll miss you all.'

'Amen to that,' said Joan.

Harriet looked around at the group, all nodding their heads sagely. They seemed to have missed the undercurrent between Gill and her. Except Katya, her eyes narrowed a little as she returned Harriet's stare.

'And yours, Harry?' she asked.

Harriet had the dreadful urge to tell all under Katya's shrewd gaze. She was closer to this group of people in lots of ways than she was with any of her girlfriends. She wanted to say there was no best, because the worst was that Gill had just signed the divorce papers and he didn't want a baby, and that she wasn't coming back because she needed a job where she could find someone who would want to have a baby with her. And she should never have come back for these two months because leaving them all had been hard enough the first time.

But she didn't. Everyone had made a concerted effort

to keep things light and she wasn't going to buck the trend. 'Being back has been so wonderful,' she said, desperately trying to eject the husky note from her voice. 'Seeing all your faces again... I missed you guys so much. That's definitely been my best.'

She paused for a while over her worst. Nimuk and the divorce were fairly good candidates but she cast around for something that would keep it light. 'I know, that two days right at the beginning where I had that V and D bug. That was terrible.'

Everyone laughed. She couldn't remember ever vomiting so hard and had certainly never slept on the floor outside her toilet because the diarrhoea had been so violent.

'You looked terrible,' said Helmut.

Harriet laughed. He was right—she had. She'd looked really bad and had felt so wretched she had just wanted to die. 'Thanks a lot.'

Harriet breathed a sigh of relief as everyone added their own colorful descriptions of her physical appearance while she'd been ill, teasing her mercilessly. The mood was light. Everyone was up again. She took a mental snapshot of the scene. In seventeen hours this chapter of her life would be closed for ever.

CHAPTER NINE

HARRIET was in her room, packing, when Gill found her. She had her door open and he watched her putting her meagre supply of clothes in her backpack. Her shoulders were slumped and despite only three metres separating them, the gap yawned widely.

He knocked softly on the door. 'An aid helicopter carrying medical personnel has been shot down not far from here. There were six on board. Kelly's gone out by road. We're preparing to accept casualties.'

'What?' Harriet couldn't believe what she was hearing. 'That's awful,' she gasped, sitting on the bed. 'I hope everyone's OK.'

Gill stayed at the door and nodded silent agreement, but he didn't hold out much hope. The likelihood of fatalities was strong and depended on many variables. He had no more information to go on. He didn't know if the helicopter had been taking off or landing, which would be better odds for the occupants, or at altitude.

Harriet felt the gloomy mood spread through her entire body. Today had been a pretty bad last day all round, and it wasn't over yet. She didn't feel remotely confident that any of the aid team had survived.

She wondered what had gone through their heads as they had plummeted to the ground. A few years ago in a different war the team had been in a chopper that had come under heavy enemy fire and it had been the most terrifying experience of her life. She had shut her eyes and gripped Gill's hand and watched a slow motion replay of her life. It had only been five minutes but it had felt like hours.

'Didn't they see the bloody great big medical aid symbol?' she asked him. The question settled into the silence. He didn't answer her and she didn't expect him to. She already knew the answer. Probably. They just hadn't cared.

It was a stark reminder that their job was dangerous, and Harriet felt a rush of bile into her throat at the thought of Gill being at risk.

'You will be careful, won't you, Gill?' she asked. Her association with him was coming to an end, and that was going to be hard, but she could deal with it as long as she knew he was safe somewhere in the world.

'Of course, Harry,' he said, as he came into the room and squatted before her. 'I'm always careful.'

Harriet snorted at him in disbelief. She had seen him take some incredible risks in their time together. 'Oh, like that time that soldier held a gun to your head to make you operate on his friend first and you turned your back on him?'

'He was a boy.' He shrugged dismissively.

'With a gun.' The worst type, as far as Harriet was concerned. Drunk on power and too young to understand how to wield it.

'He was frightened.'

'Helluva way of showing it.'

'I'll be fine, Harry,' he said, like he was talking to a patient child.

Harriet saw red. 'There's a helicopter full of people just like us that's crashed. They were just doing their job. Going about their business. Trying to help this messed-up nation. Don't tell me you'll be fine. Bet they thought they were going to be fine, too.'

This day was already turning out to be too much. She could hear the edge of hysteria in her voice and never realised before just how much safety issues weighed on her mind.

'OK, OK.' He held his arms up, surprised by the vehemence of her reaction. 'I promise I'll be careful.'

'Just play it safe, Gill. That's all I'm asking.'

He nodded at her and picked up her hand off her lap, giving it a squeeze. 'I will. Safe as houses. Now, come on.' He pulled her up off the bed as he stood. 'Let's think positive and get everything ready for six alive aid workers.'

The team adjourned to the lounge after their preparations to await news. They were tense, their conversation sporadic and stilted. They were riding the adrenaline surge that always preceded an incoming wounded situation, but the thrill of high-pressure medicine, which they all thrived on, was tempered by the knowledge that they would be operating on their own.

'How much O blood do we have?' Joan asked.

'Twenty bags,' Siobhan confirmed, not even looking up from the magazine she was feigning an interest in.

They lapsed into silence again. The ticking of the wall clock and the rustling of pages were ridiculously loud.

'Have you heard any more about your grandfather?' Helmut asked into the taut silence.

Gill shook his head. 'No. Not yet. I'll wait till I know what's happening with this first. If we're going to operate, I'll ring my father beforehand.'

Harriet had almost forgotten about Henri for a moment. She glanced at Gill guiltily. Poor man. He had enough on his mind without Henri's health to worry about.

Fifteen minutes later—almost an hour after Gill had received the news—Kelly walked into the room. She looked haggard and her scrubs were dusty with a smear of blood down the front. She pulled up a chair and raked her fingers through her hair.

'There were no survivors,' she said blankly. 'It was Peter Hanley,' she said, staring at the chipped linoleum table top.

'Damn it,' swore Gill, as an audible gasp echoed around the table. The team had worked with Peter a few years back. He was a quiet, affable Englishman. A very experienced doctor who had worked for the aid organisation for twenty-five years. He had a wife and two children.

'Bloody idiots,' said Katya, scraping her chair back. 'Bloody stupid wars.' Her accent sounded thicker, more guttural as her emotions spilled over. That was Katya. She got mad and let it out. As she banged around the kitchen, everyone stared at their hands and let her vent her anguish.

'Let's just give them all guns so they can kill each other and get it over with.' She plonked a cup of coffee in front of Kelly. 'The bad can kill the good, the good can kill the bad, and then we'll just be left with the rest of us. The sensible people. Peace-loving people.'

At another time they all might have laughed at the simplistic plan but right at this moment it seemed highly sensible. One thing Harriet had learnt from years of living in war zones was that it never made any sense. Whatever the reasons or the motives, it all still boiled down to one thing—too many senseless deaths.

The phone rang and everyone started. Their nerves had been stretched tight and the harsh mechanical noise had been unexpected.

'I'll get it,' said Gill to Joan, who had half risen. 'It might be for me.'

Joan nodded and sat back down.

'Hello, surgical building, Dr Guillaume Remy.'

Harriet knew immediately when Gill slipped into French that it was his father on the other end of the phone. Everyone waited with bated breath, eavesdropping unashamedly but unable to follow the conversation. Katya and Helmut picked up the most.

'He's stabilised,' said Gill as he hung up.

Before she could check herself, Harriet was out of her chair and folding her arms around him. She laid her head against his chest and felt the light brush of his lips on her forehead. 'Thank God,' she said.

Gill hugged her to him and squeezed her close. The relief he'd felt wash over him had been great, but sharing the moment with Harriet, with his wife who loved and knew Henri as well, was even better. She looked up at him and smiled a smile of such sweet relief he didn't question the irony of their closeness.

'When are they taking him for angiography?' Liz asked.

'If he remains stable over the next twenty-four hours, they'll take him then,' he said, running his chin absently back and forth through Harriet's soft hair, reluctant to let her go.

At least there had been a glimmer of good news on this horrible, horrible day.

CHAPTER TEN

HARRIET returned to her packing. They never brought much with them, just what could fit in a backpack. They wore scrubs all day and then got into their pyjamas. A couple of pairs of civis—jeans and T-shirts—underwear and toiletries were all they required.

Harriet always shouted herself to a few nice outfits when she hit London. After two months of blue pyjamas she needed trendy and colourful. Something in the height of fashion and completely frivolous. This time tomorrow…watch out, Knightsbridge!

Everyone else had adjourned to their rooms as well. The atmosphere was still heavy and they hadn't felt much like conversing. The mood was different to most last days and it was awkward to say the least. They wanted to be happy, they had something to celebrate, but given the circumstances it just seemed wrong to be laughing and joking and fooling around as they would normally have done. The death of Peter and the other aid workers was a far too depressing reality.

Harriet collected a few things from around the room—

a nail file on the bedside table, a notepad and pen, her digital camera. She got down on the floor on her hands and knees and put her face down against the floorboards, looking for anything that may have rolled under the bed.

Nothing. Clean as a whistle. The only thing under the bed was dust and that could most definitely stay. She rubbed her hands together to brush off the film of dust, sitting back on her haunches. She felt a stabbing pain low in the right side of her abdomen and subconsciously pressed the area with her hands. The twinge left as soon as it had come, replaced by a vague ache, which she dismissed. She'd had a couple of similar twinges over the last few days. Just another body ache and pain. She wasn't getting any younger after all.

She got up and picked up the family photos that adorned her window-sill. One was of her parents and the other was Gill with baby Thomas. Looking at the photo made her thoughts about age seem even more poignant. She was 35, her biological clock was well and truly ticking, especially with an already established sub-fertility problem.

She felt a twinge again and wondered if this month was going to be bad for her ovarian cysts. Well, why not? She hadn't had a bad month for quite a while and what was one more crappy thing to have to deal with today? She did some calculations in her head. She'd had her period two weeks ago, not that it had been much of a period, so she was coming up to mid-cycle. It was a little early but by no means unheard of for the cysts to be giving her a hard time.

As her hormones cycled through, the cysts on her one ovary would expand and grow under their influence, becoming quite large and painful. She'd even had to have one drained once via needle aspiration. Ironically, that was how they'd found out about her missing Fallopian tube and ovary. When they'd diagnosed the cysts, they'd also found her other problem.

She smiled down at the framed photo as she remembered the day it was taken. They'd had a wonderful family barbeque in their Bondi courtyard with her parents and her sister Rose and her husband Paul and, of course, baby Thomas.

He had completely unashamedly hogged the limelight. It had been a hot summer's day and they had all walked down to the beach a few hours later. Gill had been roped into making a sandcastle with his nephew. Thomas loved his Uncle Gill and that day he had tugged at Gill's hand and dragged his reluctant uncle to the paltry mound of sand he'd been constructing.

Gill had made it into a beautiful Renaissance-style château and a two-year-old Thomas had been in complete awe of it, loving his uncle all the more. She had snapped the shot of them while they hadn't been looking. Thomas had been sitting between Gill's legs, a shell poised in one hand to decorate the outer wall, and was looking up at his uncle for advice, and Gill had been pointing to the appropriate place.

Harriet loved the photo. It was hardly professional quality—the background was wrong and they weren't looking, let alone smiling, at the camera, but it was the type of photo that if her house had been burning down she'd have run back in to save. It held so many nice memories and the look of total admiration and complete and utter trust in Thomas's eyes was something she doubted any professional photo shoot would have captured. It had been a totally candid moment and she knew she would treasure it for ever.

It wasn't long after that photo had been taken that they'd

found out about Harriet's Fallopian tube and the arguments had started. She placed it in her backpack with a sigh. The photo made her feel restless…and sad, and she was already sad enough. She pushed open the French doors and walked out into the afternoon heat.

She leant against the balustrade. The sun was beginning its descent and the sky was already brilliant shades of red, gold and orange. It was a beautiful ochre sunset and she acknowledged that it was one of the things she would miss about being here. It was a land of extremes, beautiful and terrifying at the same time.

She could see the old basketball court in the distance, where a few hardy weeds struggled through the cracked, neglected concrete. She was sure that in the convent's heyday the court would have been thronged with kids, but now the deserted cement was used as the MedSurg helipad.

A dreadful noise like a siren split the air, and for a moment Harriet wondered if Kelly had pushed the incoming-wounded alarm. A rustle of movement below caught her eye and she realised it was a human wail. Nimuk's mother sat on the steps of the med building, Theire at her side, repeatedly slapping her forehead as she rocked back and forth.

Her heart-wrenching keening sounded so forlorn, so tragic that Harriet felt tears prick her eyes and got goosebumps. The grief-stricken cry rang around the cluster of buildings, announcing Nimuk's death.

There was something so base, so elementally human about the long continuous wail that it tore at the fabric of Harriet's soul. And yet there was an animal quality about it, too. It verged on demented, insane—like a wounded beast crazed with pain.

Harriet felt the tears roll down her cheeks, a stranger's

grief the key to unravelling the emotions that had been coiling tightly inside her since that morning. For once she let them flow, instead of chiding herself for being too involved. She cried for Nimuk and his mother, for Henri and Peter, for herself and Gill and the demise of their marriage, and that Gill would never sit on a beach, making sandcastles with their child. Her muted sobs were completely obliterated by the distress and torment of the grieving mother.

A few minutes later the noise stopped as abruptly as it had started and Harriet dried her tears. How many had she shed over Gill and herself these last two years? She'd lost count. It was time to stop lamenting what she couldn't have. There were worse things that could happen to a person in this world, Nimuk being a good case in point. What was her grief compared to Nimuk's mother's?

'Everything OK, Harry?'

Harriet hadn't heard Katya's approach over her own tears and the wailing mother. She shook her head, not trusting her voice, still a little too overwrought to talk. She swallowed hard against another threatening fog of emotion caused by Katya's gentle enquiry.

'Rough day?'

She nodded and cleared her throat. 'I came out to enjoy the sunset and then Nimuk's mother…'

'Da,' Katya said. 'I heard. It's very sad.'

Harriet nodded, the urge to laugh hysterically bubbling inside at Katya's typical understatement. It wasn't that Katya was unemotional—in fact, she was probably the most intensely fiery and passionate of all of them—but she'd had her release today and now she was just getting on with it.

Harriet fanned her hands in front of her face, feeling the

heat there. 'I'm sorry. I must look a state,' she said, conscious now that her eyes must be red-rimmed and her face all blotchy.

'Is this just about Nimuk?' Katya asked, her shrewd gaze doing a detailed inspection over Harriet's face. 'Are you and Gill all right?'

It was on the tip of Harriet's tongue to deny any problems. In fact, the words nearly came out before she changed her mind. She'd been sick of carrying it around by herself for two months. The sudden urge to unburden herself was intense. 'No, we're not all right. We're all wrong, actually.'

Katya nodded. 'If you don't mind me saying so, everything sounded all right this morning.'

Harriet gave a tight laugh. That morning seemed so long ago now. 'Sex has never been our problem, Katya.'

'So? What is it?'

Harriet hesitated. She didn't know how much Katya knew or had been able to piece together about her and Gill's problems. For all she knew, Gill could have kept everyone up to date. But she doubted it. Gill had always done a bit of an ostrich act and she was convinced, despite their year-long separation, that he had just been waiting for her to come to her senses so they could get on with their lives.

'I want a baby, Katya.'

'Ah.' The other woman nodded sagely. She'd known Gill long enough to know all about his vehement stance on children.

'He signed the divorce papers this morning.'

'What? What divorce papers?' asked an incredulous Katya.

Harriet was surprised at her reaction. She and Gill had

been separated for a year after all. Or was Katya like Gill, also just waiting for Harriet to come to her senses and resume her natural position, by her husband's side? Did the whole team think that, too? Had their joyous celebrations when she'd come back been because they'd been relieved she'd seen the light?

'I want a baby, Katya. He doesn't. I can't stay with him and deny myself the one thing I want more than anything.'

'Don't be ridiculous. There is more than one way to skin a cat, Harry. Just get pregnant—easy.'

Harriet gasped and felt her eyes widen at Katya's matter-of-fact solution. Although she shouldn't have been surprised. The Russian nurse was nothing if not practical. 'I could never do that, Katya! I could never trap him like that.'

'Is not trapping,' she said, being practical again. 'You are already married.'

Harriet rolled her eyes. 'No, Katya. I would never do that. Never! I want him to want to have a baby with me. Want it with every fibre of his being. I don't want to "accidentally" fall pregnant and have to live with knowing deep down that I forced Gill's hand.'

'Gill would make an excellent father,' said Katya.

'I know, I know,' Harriet agreed. 'That's what makes me so crazy. You should see him with my nephew. He's fantastic, and little Thomas just adores him. I just don't understand him.'

'Some men are just too stubborn and male to realise it. Some men need a bit of a push.'

Harriet was horrified by the conversation. Yes, right at the beginning the same evil thought had reared its ugly head, but she hadn't even considered it. That wasn't playing fair and she'd refused to stoop to such lows.

And now she was having this conversation with a woman seven years younger than her. But the really awful thing was that in her emotional state it was beginning to sound almost reasonable. She shook herself.

'I don't want any baby that he doesn't want, too, Katya.'

'So that's it? All over, red rover?'

Harriet smiled at Katya's use of Australian colloquialisms. It sounded strange in her accent. 'All over,' she whispered.

'You two are fools,' said Katya. 'Look out there.' Her arm gestured to the great dry land. 'Some people never get a chance at a love like yours. Isn't that enough to keep working at it?'

Once she would have thought so but, no, just having his love wasn't enough any more. She wanted more. Needed more. Harriet stared at her helplessly. Katya shook her head and withdrew.

Harriet knew Katya was right, but two years of wanting it had skewed it out of all proportion. She placed a hand on her stomach as the dull ache continued in her abdomen. It was a good match for the one that had taken up permanent residence in her heart.

Was she going to ache for ever?

CHAPTER ELEVEN

1700 HOURS

GILL could hear the laughter drifting out to meet him in the hallway as he strode towards the dining room. He felt relieved that everyone was laughing again. It had been a subdued couple of hours. No one looked up as he entered, engrossed as they were in their game of poker.

'Deal me in,' he said, picking up a cashew from the bowl in the centre of the table and sitting down between Harriet and Siobhan.

Harriet could feel his male heat almost instantly and wondered if there would ever be a time that his mere presence didn't have an effect on her. After seven years of being together her reactions hadn't dulled one iota. She fervently hoped there was a man somewhere out there in the world who could make her forget Gill, erase thoughts of him, sounds of him, smells of him. Or she was in serious trouble.

Gill picked up his cards and took his share of plastic chips out of Helmut's felt-lined case, and thanked God for it. It came with Helmut on every mission, even if it meant he had to sacrifice space for clothes, and had been used to while away many a boring hour.

Such was the nature of their work. Frantic hours of intense surgery, churning through a multitude of casualties, mending and patching, mending and patching. And then hours of nothing.

Not that the nothing usually went on for long. Occasionally they were blessed with a day's respite...occasionally. And it was in these down times, when they weren't catching up on their sleep, that they played poker.

He looked across at the other table. Some of Ben's team were playing Scrabble. They were quiet, concentrating intensely on their letters and the board. The others were lounging around, reading. A stark contrast to the hilarity and camaraderie of his close-knit team.

Gill couldn't help but compare the two. The difference between a team that had been together for a long time and a new one were glaringly obvious. Ben's team didn't yet have the closeness that was essential in this business. That took a while to develop but when it did, it was pure magic. And one of the many reasons he wanted to do this for ever.

Gill was conscious of Harriet beside him. He had heard Nimuk's mother a little while ago and had known how upset she would be. He had tried to resist the urge to seek her out. But it had been strange to deny such a basic instinct, stranger still that he hadn't realised how natural it was for him to play the role of her comforter. Unfortunately it was the kind of dynamic that had to stop. They were going to be divorced soon.

He assumed that eventually they'd both start new relationships, even though he knew he would never marry again. But Harriet wanted a baby—she would no doubt remarry—and while he hoped they could keep things amicable, there was such a thing as being too close. He doubted Harry's new husband would appreciate a third person in their relationship.

Anyway, he'd failed at stopping himself from going to her. He had gone to her room and seen her standing out on the balcony, and had been making his way out to her when he'd realised Katya had beaten him to it. So he had withdrawn, but not before he had heard Katya's shocking suggestion and Harriet's horrified rejection.

He didn't know how he would have reacted if Harry had deliberately set out to get pregnant. He would have been angry at being thrust into a situation he didn't want to be in, that's for sure. But realistically what could he have done? Made her terminate the baby? No—she wouldn't have done it and it wasn't something he would have asked of her. Left? No—that was more her style.

He probably would have just lumped it, but he didn't think the resentment he would feel would be at all healthy for their long-term relationship. There had to be trust in a marriage, and if he couldn't trust her then ultimately it didn't matter how much he loved her.

Helmut made a grunting, attention-seeking noise and Gill realised they were waiting for him to discard. He hadn't even looked at his cards. Oh, he'd been staring at them for long enough but his preoccupied mind hadn't registered any of them.

He caught Siobhan's gaze over the top of his cards and she winked at him. She was wearing her usual smug smile and Gill had no doubt she'd clean them all out like she usually did. Siobhan always claimed it was the luck of the Irish but Gill had a feeling that she'd been gambling since she'd first learnt to count! He'd bet his last chip she'd grown up at her father's knee. And Daddy was a bookie! Plus, she was an excellent bluffer. Her poker face was true Las Vegas—her pile of chips was already double any one else's!

A pair of kings. He tossed three cards out, holding Siobhan's unwavering gaze. He got the impression she knew exactly what he was holding in his hand. She was a card counter. He had watched her do it several times. He picked up his replacements and was careful not to give away the fact that they were rubbish. Everyone else folded. He tossed out a chip—she was not going to bluff him this time.

'Raise you another,' she said calmly.

He raised her again. She reciprocated and then so did he. Clink. Another of her chips hit the growing pile in the middle of the table.

Harriet watched them go back and forth. 'You know you're going to lose, right?' she said to him.

'Nonsense,' he dismissed jovially. 'Not with this hand.'

'Oh, yeah. Bet she's really scared,' said Katya, and they all laughed at her deadpan expression.

'Raise you another one,' Siobhan said, tossing in another chip.

'Back at ya,' he said, adding his.

'Give in, man, you can't win,' said Joan.

'Never say never,' Gill chided lightly as his chips dwindled down to the last few. The kitty was very healthy.

'I'll see you,' said Siobhan.

Damn! He'd hoped he could bluff her into folding. 'Pair of kings,' he said, with a confidence he didn't feel.

She leaned in close and whispered, 'Full house.'

The table erupted in whistles and cheers as Siobhan all but cleaned Gill out. Helmut gave her a high five.

They kept playing for a while longer. Gill won back some of his chips, mainly from Harriet who was particularly hopeless at poker, but Siobhan had them all cleaned out within half an hour.

Helmut threw his cards on the table in frustration. 'How does she do that?' he asked no one in particular.

Just then they heard a muffled explosion. It was off somewhere in the distance, not close but not too far away either. Several more followed in short succession.

The atmosphere changed abruptly. There was tension now among the group, alertness. Cards remained unshuffled, magazines unread, Scrabble tiles untouched as they strained their ears and listened in silence to the popping of distant gunfire and the crump of explosions that continued unabated. It sounded like fireworks but they all knew it wouldn't be remotely pretty when the wounded started to arrive.

Harriet shuddered. It was a sound she'd never got used to. She glanced at Gill. His reaction was different. She could see the surgeon appearing before her eyes. She could see him calculating arrival times and operating schedules, priming himself for action. He was so cut out for this type of work. How could she ask him to leave it?

'We'd better eat something,' said Gill. 'No telling when we'll next get the chance.'

CHAPTER TWELVE

1800 HOURS

THE incoming-wounded siren wailed across the complex as they were tucking into their reheated frozen dinners. Harriet knew it was coming, the noises of war hadn't stopped for over half an hour, but the siren was at just the right pitch. It made her jump every time.

'Twelve more hours,' muttered Katya to no one in particular. 'Couldn't they have waited twelve more hours to kill each other?'

'Apparently not,' said Helmut, pushing away his half-eaten dinner.

Gill scraped his chair back and walked over to the ringing wallphone near the door.

'Kelly? What's the story?'

He nodded a lot and said 'Mmm' a lot and then replaced the receiver. 'The first wave will be arriving in the next fifteen minutes. We should expect the first patient in half an hour.'

The two teams took in Gill's statement in silence. No one got up or rushed and hurried around. The theatres were still set to go from the helicopter crash earlier so all they needed were the patients. Instead, they took a moment to have some silent reflection, mental preparation for the next few gruelling hours.

Gill wondered if they would still be operating in the morning when their flight was supposed to be leaving. It had happened before. One chopper had flown in with two replacement teams, an hour had been scheduled for handover then the same chopper had flown out an hour later with the two incumbent teams. But Gill had never thought it fair on the newbies to have to hit the ground running, and knew he wouldn't leave the operating theatre until the victims of this latest skirmish had all been dealt with. The helicopter would just have to wait.

Still with his grandfather weighing heavily on his mind and a certain degree of urgency over returning home, he hoped there wouldn't be too many bodies to put back together again. He smiled at the analogy. That's what they were—all the king's horses and all the king's men. Putting soldiers and civilians alike back together. Unfortunately for some, like poor Humpty, no amount of surgical intervention would make a difference.

Harriet felt nauseated. There was nothing new in that. The moment the siren wailed, a surge of adrenaline hit her bloodstream and her body responded in kind. Her heart beat loudly in her chest, its tempo picking up as each second ticked by. And her stomach prepared for fright or flight by immediately wanting to evacuate its contents. She swallowed against the rising urge. As Gill had said, there was no telling when they would next eat.

She'd never realised how much she dreaded the adrenaline response until now. It was a fairly basic human reaction to stressful situations and she knew that for the next how ever many hours it would be adrenaline that kept her on her toes, anticipating Gill's needs, keeping one step ahead.

But afterwards was awful. Coming down from the high, the buzz, was the terrible part. She hated the shaky, strung-out feeling. How everything around her seemed far away and a fog blanketed her brain, making her thoughts slower and her tongue feel all thick and fat in her mouth. Coming down off the high was not at all pleasant and the only consolation was that at least she'd be *en route* to London when it hit. She found London was generally a good antidote to the withdrawal. To most things, actually.

The dull ache in her side was still there and she contemplated taking some pain killers. It wasn't exactly painful but as it twinged again she knew she couldn't afford to have it interfere with the hours of surgery ahead. A couple of tablets usually did the trick.

She rose as the teams were quietly talking about the possible injuries and walked into the kitchen area. A first-aid kit beneath the sink carried basic medication. It was a hard plastic contraption that consisted of a series of little drawers. Each drawer had its contents written on it. She located the tablets, pushed two out of the blister pack and popped them in her mouth, swallowing them down with some bottled water.

'Are you OK?'

Gill's deep voice was right near her ear and she could feel his heat directly behind her. It was so tempting to lean back into him. She clutched the sink to stop herself from swaying back.

'Sure,' she said, turning around, forcing him to take a step back. 'Just a little niggle.'

'A niggle? Where?'

'It's fine, Gill,' she said, massaging her side absently. 'I think I have another cyst building.'

'Oh…OK.' He stood there feeling worse than useless. She had been badly troubled by the cysts over the years and he had seen her in quite a bit of pain, but he didn't know what she expected of him any more. Was he supposed to make a fuss or just nod and let her get on with it?

Any conversation they could get into now seemed fraught with problems. He'd been down this road before and knew it was scattered with landmines. Talking about her cysts led to talking about her ovary and then her Fallopian tube and then her fertility and then her desire for a baby. They had a few minutes before critically injured patients depended on them and he knew he couldn't go into the operating theatre on the back of an argument.

He needed clarity. They could potentially be operating well into the night, if not all night. It was important to not be distracted by external forces. He couldn't bring his re-lationship problems into the operating theatre. One wrong move could be potentially fatal or lengthen the operating time significantly.

And this was a true pressure cooker. Get them in, get them out, move them on. If he allowed himself to be distracted to the point where mistakes were made, the process slowed and things got backed up. And potentially people died.

Maybe that was why he had spent the last year so success-fully in denial. He'd been able to spend so much time shutting down any thoughts of his crumbling marriage out of neces-sity. Maybe that was why the papers this morning had come as a surprise. Maybe they shouldn't have, but they had.

'Let me know if it gets worse,' he said.

'It'll be fine, Gill.' Harriet tried and failed to keep the

irritation out of her voice. The adrenaline was making her edgy. He was going to be proprietorial now? She didn't need him to take care of her. She'd been managing just fine without him.

Gill heard the terseness in his voice and felt a little annoyed himself. 'I can't afford to have one of my team not at a hundred per cent. If you're going to scrub in, I need you to be on top of your game.'

Harriet glared at her husband. How dared he call her professionalism into question? 'When have I ever not been on my game?' she demanded.

Gill realised too late that he'd somehow managed to get himself into an argument anyway. If he could have bitten his tongue off, he would have. He truly didn't need this now. Now was the time for mental preparation. To ride the wave of adrenaline to his advantage. Hone his instincts, sharpen his vision, tune up his mental abilities.

'Look, I'm sorry…you're right. I worry about you, Harry.'

'Really?' She raised delicately arched brows.

'Yes. Despite everything, you are still my wife. Your problems are my problems.'

'Well, don't worry, Gill,' she said sweetly, her face aching with the effort it took to keep a saccharine-sweet smile there. 'Pretty soon they won't be yours to worry about and you won't have to worry about me being off my game.' She pushed herself away from the sink, their arms brushing as she strode away.

Gill sighed. Great! Well done, there, old chap. The phone rang and he strode across the room and picked it up on the third ring.

He listened for a brief second. 'Shrapnel to the abdomen,' he said to Ben.

'I'll take it.' Ben nodded and his team rose to do their duty.

'I wonder if the patient was one of the bastards that shot Peter out of the sky?' said Katya, again to no one in particular.

Harriet stopped her finger drumming on the table and looked at her friend. They all did. Katya had summed up in one sentence the conundrum of their job. They tried to forget that a lot of their patients were the bad guys. It wasn't their job to pick and choose who they operated on and the backgrounds of the people who came through their doors didn't matter—everyone got the same treatment, the same surgical options.

But Peter's death and the unfairness of it all still weighed on their minds. Katya's statement wouldn't be far from their thoughts as they operated tonight.

The phone rang again and Gill snatched it up before it had a chance to ring again. 'Yes?'

Gill looked tense and Harriet felt churlish for arguing with him. He should be looking primed, instead he looked on edge. No doubt she had thrown a real spanner in the works of the mental preparation she knew he went through every time the siren wailed. Still, knowing Gill, it wouldn't take him long to get back into his groove.

'Female with a pneumothorax, needing a Caesar,' Gill announced. 'She's 35 weeks and the baby's in foetal distress.'

The team didn't move for a second, no doubt all a little stunned. Harriet couldn't ever remember the team ever being asked to perform a C-section. She didn't even want to think about the personal irony of it all.

'Well, come on, guys,' said Gill, a sharp edge to his voice. 'We have to get this baby out.'

They moved then, spurred by the urgency in Gill's

voice. He watched them troop out. Harriet was last and he grabbed her arm. 'I'm sorry, Harry.'

She nodded. The note of sincerity was obvious. 'A baby, Gill? How ironic.' And she turned on her heel.

Gill shut his eyes momentarily and leaned his head against the wall. He waited for the familiar rise of adrenaline to kick his system into hyperdrive but it didn't come. He sighed in frustration. What the hell was wrong with him today? Too much on his mind, damn it! Suddenly he'd rather be curled up on his lounge in Bondi with Harriet than about to pull a wet and bawling baby out of its nice soft home. Hell! He never felt like this.

He blamed the events of the day. It had certainly been eventful! The divorce and his grandfather and Nimuk and Peter and arguing with Harriet. And now…a baby!

CHAPTER THIRTEEN

1900 HOURS

IT WAS Harriet's turn to scrub in. She almost passed. She almost said to Siobhan and Katya that she would circulate again but a stubborn brain cell somewhere refused to let Gill off the hook. He was going to have to look her in the eye as he passed the baby to her and she would meet his gaze with a silent challenge in hers.

It would say, You, too, could have this. You, too, could create human life and rejoice in it and make a real contribution to this world. Yes, you do that already, but this is so much more personal. This is about fulfilling your biological purpose, truly becoming what you were born to become. A father.

She left Katya and Siobhan setting up as she tied her mask in place and flicked the taps on. She ripped open a sterile pre-soaped sponge and began her thorough three-minute surgical scrub. She started at her fingertips, paying special attention to her nail beds, and worked her way down the fingers to the palms and backs of her hands.

Gill joined her and began his scrub at the sink beside her. She ignored him as much as she could ignore possibly one of the most gorgeous men on the planet, and continued working the sponge down, scrubbing at her wrists and further still until all the way down to her elbows was now sterile. She held her soapy arms upright in front of her as she put them back under the tap and let water and soap sluice off her arms, running from her fingertips and dripping off her elbows.

Harriet shut off the tap with a push of her elbow and stood still for a moment, waiting for the elbow dripping to settle. She flapped her arms a little to hasten the process.

As she departed, her arms still upright, Gill said, 'Did the paracetamol help?'

'Yes, thank you.' It had, actually. The niggle was noticeable when she moved, but had practically all but disappeared otherwise. But she would have said yes even if it hadn't been the case. She wouldn't have given him the satisfaction of being right.

Harriet turned before she got to the swing doors that led into the theatre, pushing them open with her back and bottom and then swinging round so she was facing forward again as they swished shut behind her. Katya had set up a trolley for them, where they could dry their hands on sterile towels and then gown and glove. Harriet had her gown on and was just finishing gloving when Gill entered the theatre in the same way she had.

She moved away from the trolley as Gill approached and busied herself over by the operating table, opening packs and sorting her instruments, asking for Betadine to be poured into one of the metal bowls and doing a swab and instrument count with Siobhan. She checked the suction.

The silence in the theatre was broken as Joan and Helmut

wheeled a hysterical woman inside. She was crying and moaning and Theire was talking calmly to her. Harriet felt goose-bumps break out beneath the long sleeves of the gown at the cries that needed no interpreting. It was patently obvious as the scared woman clutched at her abdomen that she was terrified over the welfare of her baby.

Harriet felt her own abdomen twinge again and it felt as if her only ovary was responding to the young mother's plight. She couldn't be much more than twenty, thought Harriet, and the ugly tube hanging out of one side of her chest to reinflate her lung was probably more than enough for her to deal with. How had this young woman got caught up in the fighting? Like they all had, Harriet guessed— wrong place, wrong time.

Theire explained as the vocal woman shuffled over onto the operating table that Joan was going to put her to sleep and when she woke up she would have a beautiful baby. Harriet kept her fingers crossed that it would be the case and they didn't encounter any complications.

The woman's cries petered out as Joan injected an an-aesthetic agent into her IV.

'Let's go,' said Gill.

Joan intubated the woman and had her hooked up to monitors and ready to go in five minutes. Harriet passed Gill the green drapes one at a time until the woman com-pletely disappeared beneath the drapes and they had a large, sterile operative field.

Joan nodded at Gill, indicating that everything was good to begin.

'Prep,' he said.

Harriet passed him the bowl of Betadine and a swab on a stick. He dipped the swab into the dark brown liquid and liberally applied it to the woman's abdomen. Gill opened his mouth to ask for the scalpel and found it in his hand before he could even get the word out.

'Thank you, Harry,' he murmured, and there was a brief moment when their gazes met above their masks and he saw a flash of the old Harriet. The one he'd been happily married to for five years before she'd changed the plot on him. The one who could anticipate his needs in an operating theatre better than anyone else he had worked with. He missed that Harriet.

Ella came on, singing Mack the Knife, and Gill almost smiled at the appropriateness as he made a horizontal incision low, just above the woman's pubic bone. A horizontal incision would have made for easier access but just because this young woman probably wasn't going to be wearing a bikini ever didn't mean she didn't deserve as much consideration to her body image as Western women who thought C-sections were a designer choice.

Blood welled up from the incision and he mopped it up with towels and used diathermy on the bleeding points. The smell of burnt flesh permeated his mask. He quickly achieved a bloodless field and could see the pink colour of the stretched uterus.

Next he made a similar shallow incision into the uterine wall and took the blunt dissection instrument Harriet gave him and slowly opened up the incision further, making it wider and deeper with each separation of the uterine fibres. He stopped when he saw the membranes glistening like a peeled grape.

'Ready for the suction,' he said out of habit, but as he glanced down he noticed Harriet was poised with the sucker in hand. He used the scalpel again to pierce through the two membranes. As the clear, sweet-smelling amniotic fluid spouted out of the hole, Harriet efficiently sucked it all away.

Harriet could feel her heartbeat starting to pick up. Any second now Gill was going to pull the baby, hopefully kicking and screaming, out of its comfortable home. He would place it in her arms, and maybe for one or two seconds she could pretend that it was their baby he was giving to her.

Gill used his gloved fingers to tear the membranes open. 'Come on, little one. Time for the big bad world,' he said, supporting the head as he gently eased the baby out through the incision. Gill felt the team's collective breath hold as he laid the silent newborn down on the drapes and sucked her nose and mouth with a catheter Harriet had passed him. He was conscious of her clamping and cutting the cord as he cleared the baby's airways.

The baby girl did not like it one little bit and a lusty wail and flailing fists were the response to the potent stimulus. Harriet felt tears prick her eyes at the joyous noise and felt rather than heard the collective sigh of relief.

'What a beautiful noise,' said Helmut, as Joan passed him the syntocin to inject into the woman's IV to aid the expulsion of the placenta.

Until you have to wake up to it every night at 2 a.m., thought Gill as he picked up the wet, bawling infant and prepared to hand her over to Harriet. He noticed the re-proah in her gaze as she held out her green-drape-covered arms. He felt as if she'd read his mind.

But then something happened. As he passed the infant down into Harriet's waiting arms he had a flash of what it would be like to be passing their newborn to her, still wet from its birth.

The bundle he was holding suddenly felt very precious and he eased the baby girl ever so gently into his wife's arms and watched as she stared at the child's face with utter fascination. Harriet rocked the baby gently as she wrapped the little one in the green cloth to keep her warm. The baby's cries quietened and he watched more than a little fascinated himself as the woman and child blinked at each other.

Harriet looked up at Gill again with wonder in her eyes and he felt a twinge of something deep inside. He didn't know what it was, but he did know she looked so beautiful with that look in her eyes, even through the layers of theatre clothes and her face obscured by a mask, and he wanted to be responsible for putting that look there again.

Holding the child, gazing into her husband's eyes, Harriet had to stop herself from speaking out loud. *Please. Please, Gill. This is what I want. A baby. Your baby. Don't you see how wonderful and precious they are? Look at how she's looking at me like I'm the most important thing in the entire world. Where else can you get that? Knowing you are someone's everything, that somebody out there truly loves you unconditionally?*

Katya cleared her throat behind Harriet and broke the intense gaze between the two. Harriet reluctantly handed the baby over to Katya, who also had her arms draped with a sterile towel so that Harriet wouldn't contaminate herself. She wished there was a paediatrician standing by to give the baby the once-over, especially as the babe was a little on the premature side, but this was a war zone. They made do with what they had. Thankfully the baby hadn't required any resuscitation.

Harriet watched as Joan assumed the paediatric role and, satisfied, turned back to concentrate on the continuing operation. Gill was performing a controlled cord traction, gently pulling on the thick, rope-like structure to ease the placenta out. It came away and Harriet presented him with a kidney dish. He placed the placenta in the metal container and Harriet turned and passed it to Katya.

'Large swab,' said Gill, as he eased the now deflated uterus out of the mother's body.

Harriet passed him the thin but absorbent cloth with the radio-opaque strip down the centre. He spread it out over his open hand, inserted his hand into the uterus via the incision and did a sweep of the inside to ensure no products had been left behind.

Satisfied that all seemed in order, he asked Harriet for a suture so he could close. She passed it to him and he listened to her and Siobhan doing a count as he began his layered closure.

CHAPTER FOURTEEN

HARRIET, Katya and Siobhan were cleaning up as Gill accompanied the mother and baby back to the medical building. They weren't HDU candidates and they didn't require evacuation either so it was back to Kelly and her teams.

The battle was still intense in the distance as Gill and Megan pushed the trolley along the concrete pathway that connected the two buildings. There was no lighting so Gill was thankful for the gentle kiss of the full moon.

'There's a bit of a lull at the moment,' Kelly said, as she accepted the patient from Gill. 'I sent Ben a compound scrub of a fractured tib and fib. The leg was pretty messed up. There weren't too many badly injured in this first lot but, as you can hear…' she indicated over her shoulder to the noise still raging outside '…it's not over yet. Next batch arriving in about half an hour.'

Gill watched as Kelly took the baby from Megan and made cooing noises at the little bundle. He rolled his eyes. Funny, seeing Kelly with the baby didn't have the same effect as having seen Harriet with her. Now he could view the baby as a cute but tragic part of war. But for a little while back in the theatre, with Harriet by his side looking at him with those big brown eyes, he hadn't been so distant.

'Biological clock ticking, Kelly?' he teased.

'Women's clocks are always ticking, Guillaume. It's just that we become more in tune with it. Who wouldn't want one of these little darlings?' she said, rubbing her nose against the baby's forehead. 'You and Harry thinking of having a baby?'

Gill laughed the question off. He wished he had a dollar for every time they'd been asked since they'd got married when they were going to start a family. Up until two years ago their standard reply had been that they liked their family of two and were too selfish to share, but a lot had changed in a couple of years.

Most people had been horrified by their assertion that babies were not on their agenda, including both sets of parents and especially Gill's grandfather. But he and Harriet had remained unswayed, happy to remain childless.

This notion had been reaffirmed many a time when one by one their friends had succumbed to their biological urges and one by one had dropped out of sight. Too tired to come to dinner. Too tired to have a coherent conversation. And even when it had been managed, it had usually been one of those frustrating broken dialogues constantly interrupted by a crying baby or an insistent toddler.

No, their DINK lifestyle was much cherished. Or so he'd thought.

A large milky white moon hung from the relentless blackness of the night sky and blanketed the harsh landscape in its glow, softening the ferocity of the desolate terrain. As Harriet scrubbed the used instruments at the sink at the back of the theatre, she stared absently at the view out the window. There was a strange beauty to the austerity and it was easy to forget that bad things were happening here.

She looked at the moonlight coating the ancient soil and felt very small and insignificant. Even in a country as divided as this, life still went on. All around, the cycle of life inched onward with glacial patience. Men and women fell in love, babies were born, wars were fought. The barely perceptible forward motion of life made her feel like a tiny cog in a very big wheel.

She had seen the good and bad of the cycle today. The highs and lows. She thought back to how devastated she'd felt only hours ago, witnessing Nimuk's precarious hold on life and his mother's anguish as he'd lost the struggle, and how death and life were intimate partners in a never-ending cycle. Someone died. And someone was born. It was the way of the world and in this big troubled land the cycle was relentless.

She returned her attention to the job at hand. The instruments had to be thoroughly scrubbed to remove any blood or tissue traces before they went into the steriliser. Katya and Siobhan were on the other side of the door, prepping for their next case—wiping surfaces down with a chlorhexedine solution, getting out gowns and gloves and basic packs—and she was feeling restless after the C-section so scrubbing metal objects gave her something useful to do with her hands.

Harriet's heart fluttered madly every time she thought about Gill passing the newborn baby to her. She could have sworn he had been affected by the experience, too, and her heart leapt at the encouraging step forward. Too little, too late, Harriet, she lectured herself. And she knew it was but, oh, what a buzz!

Gill found her a few minutes later, rinsing the cleaned instruments in the sink. He observed her quietly from the doorway as she rattled them around for a bit and then stopped to stare out the window for a long moment.

'Penny for them,' he said softly, and heard her sigh as she turned slightly towards him.

She shrugged. Did she blurt out what she'd been thinking about just now? Tell him she knew how affected he'd been during the C-section and how just thinking about it had her heart hammering like a teenager before her first kiss?

'Just thinking about nature. The cycle of life. One baby dies. Another one is born. Nimuk dies and a little girl is born. Don't you ever feel small and insignificant? Like we're all just part of one great master plan? Or is that just last-day blues?' She gave a self-deprecating smile and turned back to the instruments.

'You always get reflective on the last day.'

'Do I?' she asked, surprised, turning back again.

He nodded. Her face was now mask-less and even though her hair was hidden in the cap, the moonlight streaming through the window behind her framed her beautifully. She looked like an exotic part of the ageless landscape that had infiltrated the glass and stepped into the building.

'You forget, Harry, I know you. We can separate and even divorce but I'll always be your guy. I'll always be the man who knows you best.'

Harriet didn't doubt it for a moment. Maybe when she remarried and she and her husband had been together for many years, maybe then she could tell him he was wrong. But until then Gill was, as he had put it, her guy. He did know her and understand her better than anyone.

'Then you know that holding that baby affected me.

And I'm pretty sure it affected you, too. Don't you forget that I also know you.'

Gill rubbed his hands through his hair, removing his cap as he did so. 'Yes, OK, for a moment I did think about a baby. About our baby. But…I'm sorry, I wish I could adequately explain why I don't feel the urge to pro-create—I just don't. Kelly was holding the baby before and all I could see was an unfortunate victim of war. The…stuff I felt in Theatre when you were holding her just wasn't there. I didn't feel anything. I suspect it had more to do with you than the baby. And you know, maybe when I'm fifty, when I'm old and grey, maybe I'll regret not having children. But I'm fairly at one with the decision now.'

'It'll be too late to do anything about it when you are old and grey.'

'I can live with that, Harry.'

Harriet felt the years of their disagreement well up between them again. She almost cried in frustration. She'd been through all this and had made a decision, but she could feel herself being sucked into the same old argument again. Trying to convince him he was wrong. Trying to make him see.

For a brief moment during the C-section she'd thought he'd finally got it. And somewhere inside him a little light was dawning. But he was still letting his preconceived ideas suffocate the fledgling glimmer of light, and she didn't have time to hang around and wait for him to get it. If, indeed, that was even possible.

'Here you both are,' said Siobhan, bustling through the swing door, oblivious to the atmosphere.

Harriet turned back to the sink and began sorting

through the instruments, packing them back inside the stainless-steel tray and grouping them neatly. Her side was really starting to ache now.

'How's the little one going?' Siobhan asked.

Gill rolled his eyes. Suddenly every female within range was clucky! 'Fine,' he said in an I'm-going-to-humour-you voice. He noticed Harriet still had her back to them.

'Katya and I were talking and we decided we should give her a name.'

Harriet turned at the suggestion. Yes, that's exactly what they should do. 'Oh, yes!' she exclaimed. 'What a great idea.'

Gill looked from one to the other. 'Ah, guys...I think it's traditional for the mother to name the child.'

'Don't be obtuse,' she rebuffed him good-naturedly in her lilting Irish accent. 'How many times in these situations do you get to see such a positive side to life? We see too much death and dying. It's nice to see new life for a change. How many C-sections have you done with MedSurg?'

'Counting this one? One.'

'Precisely. We need to celebrate life. Don't you think so, Harry?'

'Yes,' she said, her chin rising as she looked him square in the face, 'we do.'

'Well, great, we'll all drink too much champagne on the flight home tomorrow. Naming the child isn't necessary. For a start it'll have its own name and secondly we'll never see her again. What's the point?'

'The point?' asked Harriet, as another cramping pain gnawed at her side. 'The point is that names are important. I know you surgeons have difficulty remembering that, but they're what humanise us. It's how we're identified. And each one tells a story about the person and the origin of their birth.

'Like your name, for example. Your Australian mother wanted a French name to remind you of your heritage but your French dad wanted you to fit in so he wanted an English name. They compromised, christening you with the French version of William but settling on calling you Gill for short. Your grandfather is the only one who calls you by your proper name.

'See, Gill? A name's not just what someone calls you to get your attention. It says so much about your family and your history. It contains your story. That's important. And so was this birth, and I think Siobhan is right. When we talk about this night in years to come, we'll be able to talk about the baby by name. It'll make it that much more special.'

Gill and Siobhan stared wordlessly at her for a few moments. 'Yep,' said Siobhan, 'what she said.'

'Are you OK?' Gill asked.

Harriet frowned at him. She'd been so deep in concentration she hadn't realised she'd had her hand on her hip and was absently massaging her abdomen.

'Fine,' she dismissed briskly, dropping her hand.

Gill sighed and looked back at Siobhan. 'OK, we name the baby. Any suggestions?'

'Kat,' said Katya as she joined the conversation, and everyone laughed.

Harriet felt Katya's watchful gaze on her. She raised her own gaze and smiled reassuringly at her friend.

'What about Caesar, after the way she was bought into the world?' said Siobhan.

'Too masculine,' said Gill.

Harriet blinked in surprise. For someone who was reluctant to get involved, he was being very sensitive to the process. 'Gillian,' she said. It was perfect. 'Name her after Gill, the doctor who brought her into the world.'

'Oh, yes.' Siobhan clapped her hands together excitedly. 'That's perfect Harry.'

'Gillian...Gillian,' said Katya, rolling it around her tongue a couple of times before nodding her agreement.

'No, no,' said Gill, holding his hands up. 'We were all there. It was a team effort.'

'Yes,' insisted Harriet firmly. 'Yours was the first face she ever saw. Do you know how special that is? You're connected. Whether you like it or not.'

Harriet liked it. She liked it a lot. Gillian wasn't his child. She wasn't their child. But somewhere in this world Gill was connected with a baby and she couldn't think of a better memory to take away from her last day.

CHAPTER FIFTEEN

'BURR holes for probable extradural haematoma,' said Gill, putting down the phone. 'It's on its way over.'

The chatter about the newly named baby died down. And Gill was extremely grateful to be getting his team back to work. Even Helmut had been gaga over the baby...over Gillian. He supposed he couldn't really blame them. It was something very different to what they usually dealt with and, as Siobhan had said, after a decade of dealing in trauma and hatred and death, it was exciting to be a part of life. To celebrate the beginning of life instead of mourning the end or trying to avoid it. Or at the very least delaying it.

Harriet went back to the outside room and put a tray of neuro instruments into the steriliser. It was a portable unit that used steam and heat to disinfect surgical instruments. It had two shelves so two trays could be sterilised at any one time.

It was quite an old machine, heavy and metallic, rarely used in modern theatres any more, but it did the job. Pop them in, shut the door, turn the wheel to seal the unit, turn it on and a few minutes at maximum heat and pressure and, bingo! Sterile instruments.

The important thing to remember was to release the pressure valve and not to open the heavy door until the pressure had come back down to zero. Her student nurse days had been filled with horror stories about nurses who had been killed by heavy pressurised doors blowing out and hitting them square in the chest.

Between that and watching the graphic film *Hospitals Don't Burn Down* that all students had to watch, Harriet had seen hazards around every corner. As long as she lived she'd never forget the scene where the nurse opened the linen chute on the top floor and the fire, which had started in the bowels of the hospital, tunnelled up the chute seeking a new oxygen supply, and sprayed out at her, killing her instantly.

Harriet shuddered, thinking about it now as she shut off the pressure valve. She supposed it had achieved its aim—fire awareness. She'd always been really careful and very watchful for potential fire sources. Vigilant was a good word. She'd even received an award at their end-of-training dinner for the nurse most likely to single-handedly evacuate an entire hospital in the case of fire.

She had laughed and graciously accepted the beat-up old trophy someone had found at the dump of a fireman carrying a person in his arms. But deep down she'd hoped that her mettle would never be tested.

Even at home in their Bondi unit she had insisted that they have a fire extinguisher, smoke detectors in every room and a fire blanket in the kitchen. Gill had always teased her, calling her his very own fire warden.

He'd bought her a fireman's hat for Christmas one year, although, as she'd found out, it had had little to do with fire and everything to do with wanting her to wear it to bed and indulge in a little role playing. That hadn't worked for her but on him...now, that had definitely worked!

Harriet blinked as she realised where her thoughts were heading and roused herself from the past. She removed the tray from the steriliser, using a long-handled, angled instrument designed exactly for the job, and took care not to contaminate any of the instruments. She plonked the tray down on a sterile towel she had laid out and waited a couple of minutes for the steam to evaporate and for the instruments to cool off.

And for her to cool off. She didn't want to walk into the theatre and have to look at Gill when a vivid memory of him in a fireman's hat and nothing else had her shaking all over—despite the pain in her side. They'd had so many good times, laughed so much. She knew it would be so easy to go to him and tear up the divorce papers and be with him and love him for the rest of her life.

But something would always be missing. Gillian had brought it glaringly to the fore again. Just because he looked magnificent in a fireman's hat drawling 'Ma'am' at her, it wasn't a good enough reason to sacrifice her wants and needs. She knew she could keep Gill happy but she also knew he couldn't do the same for her.

'Here she is,' said Siobhan to Katya, as Harriet schooled her features into neutrality and entered the theatre.

'Sorry,' said Harriet.

'Is OK,' said Katya.

Bless you, thought Harriet. Katya had known that she had needed some time to herself. Once again she realised how much she was going to miss these people.

The patient was already in the theatre and had been intubated by Kelly for decreased level of consciousness.

Helmut was looking after his airway and hyperventilating him with mechanical breaths from a black bag attached to his tube. Hyperventilation was an important part of head-injury management. The theory was that carbon dioxide, a known potent cerebral vasodilator, was blown off, thus preventing excess cerebral blood flow and keeping intra-cranial pressure down.

Gill and Joan were looking at the patient's X-ray on the viewing box. Harriet saw the fracture of his left temporal bone.

'So we're not sure if he has an extradural, right?' asked Harriet, joining them.

'Can't be sure without a CT scan,' said Gill. 'All we can go on is the clinical picture. Kelly said he'd been complaining of a headache and weakness in his right arm and leg after sustaining a blow to the head with a rifle butt. They did a skull X-ray and found the fracture then he rapidly lost consciousness and blew his left pupil. She tubed him then.'

Harriet nodded, looking at their patient. Sounded like a typical cranial bleed picture. So they were going to have a drill a hole in his head and hope they could find the blood clot and evacuate it. If not, the patient's problems were probably a lot more severe and, as Gill had said, without a CT, impossible to know for sure.

'He looks so young,' said Harriet, still not yet numbed to the fact that teenagers fought wars.

'Fits with the extradural picture.' Joan nodded.

Gill scrubbed, taking his time to be thorough, despite the urgency. The last thing this young man needed was for him to introduce a pathogen directly into his brain. Burr-hole surgery could be quite successful and reverse poten-tially bad outcomes. If there was some blood between the skull and the dura, the first of three layers of protection around the brain, then removing it should be relatively easy. The patient certainly didn't need his recovery hindered by a dose of meningitis.

Gill hoped as he concentrated on his scrub that he located the blood with his first burr hole. He was more than aware that the patient might not have an extradural at all, although he'd bet his last cent on it. They were embarking on a fishing expedition inside someone's head and once he started he'd have to make several attempts to either find it or satisfy himself that there was nothing to be found.

Gill had done many of these procedures over the years and was more than conscious of the fact that the object of this type of emergency surgery was to decompress the head and then get the patient out to specialised help. Drill a hole, evacuate the blood, stitch him up and fly him out. Not drill as many holes as he could and fluff around till he found something.

The other possibility was that he'd find a subdural hae-matoma—blood underneath the dural covering. Gill sin-cerely hoped not. It wasn't that he couldn't handle it, it was just a little longer, a little more complicated, a little more potentially serious for the patient.

'Mannitol's finished,' said Helmut to Gill, as Gill entered the theatre with wet arms held up in front of him. Good, that should deal with any cerebral oedema caused by the pressure of the blood clot on the surrounding tissues. Now, to find it…

Harriet and Helmut positioned the patient on the table as Gill gowned and gloved. They propped a doughnut headrest beneath the young man's head and a sandbag beneath his left shoulder to help keep his head averted to the right. Harriet heard the buzz of hair clippers and watched as Helmut shaved half the patient's head, noting the boggy swelling above the temple and a slight graze where the assault had occurred.

'Remind me to never let you cut my hair,' murmured Harriet, and Helmut winked at her.

'Ready, Joan?' asked Gill.

'You may proceed,' she chirped in a fake high-society accent and then laughed self-deprecatingly.

Gill prepped the shaved area with Betadine and Harriet hit the play button on the CD player. Ella was on, Joan was happy and, apart from the now constant niggle in her side, Harriet cruised happily into circulating mode.

This was the part she really enjoyed about her job. Watching Gill operate. Seeing his brow pucker in concentration, his long fingers accept instruments with practised ease, his quick mind and skilled hands anticipating and adapting.

She loved standing beside him and watching him up close but sometimes she almost preferred watching him from a distance. She could observe without the sheer force of his physical presence blurring her senses. He was at home in his scrubs and with his hands inside someone's body. This was his environment. Watching him was like watching an artist paint or a songwriter compose lyrics— it was pure poetry in motion.

Gill made a vertical incision about three centimetres long over the swollen fracture site. It was no lower than the cheekbone to avoid cutting the facial nerve, and one finger's-breadth in front of the tragus of the ear. He separated the temporalis muscle and incised the periosteum, inserting a self-retaining retractor and cauterising a couple of bleeding blood vessels.

He could now see the white skull bone. 'Drill,' he said, and Katya passed it to him.

The drill was a manual device, which looked almost exactly like a standard hand-operated wood drill. They used much more modern expensive pneumatic drills in large operating theatres but the old-fashioned drill still did the job. He slowly cranked the handle round and round to make a hole through the bone, careful not to use too much pressure and accidentally plunge through into the brain.

He felt an irregular wobbling and pulled back, knowing that he had perforated through the two to three millimetres of temporal bone. The hole was too small to tell if there was any extradural blood. 'Conical burr, please.' Gill needed to enlarge the hole to be sure.

'There she blows,' he said, as the haematoma became evident. He relaxed a little. Finding the bleed straight away was a relief. He hadn't wanted to drill any more holes but wouldn't have been able to avoid it had the first one been negative. He would have had to keep going, making more holes until either he'd found it or he could be reasonably certain there wasn't a bleed to be found.

'Ronguer, please.' Gill used the heavy bone-cutting scissors to nibble away a little extra bone and expose more of the haematoma. Katya passed him a syringe and he gently washed out the rather large blood clot and cauterised the bleeding point.

'OK, let's get this kid out of here,' said Gill as he prepared to close.

Harriet blinked as a rush of faintness washed over her. She leaned back against the wall and watched as Gill expertly brought the muscle and skin layers together again, using staples for the external incision. She wasn't humming along to Ella as she usually did, though. In fact, she was forcing herself to concentrate on what he was doing and ignore the sudden surge of nausea that was trying to outdo the cyst pain for her attention.

'Pupils are equal and reacting,' said Joan, flashing a penlight in her patient's eyes. 'Well done, Guillaume. Good save. I've given him some broad-spectrum antibiotic cover,' she said.

Gill thanked her as he placed the last staple, pulling his gloves and gown off, looking for Harriet and catching a glimpse of her as she slipped out through the doors. He didn't realise he did that until now. Until she wasn't there. Looked at her for that smile in her eyes that said, You did good, you're my hero. Even after a year's separation she had still given him that look post-op. He'd got back into the habit of expecting it and realised he was going to have to get out of the habit all over again.

Harriet pulled the lid down on the toilet and sat on it with wobbly legs. She wiped her mouth with the back of her hand, the acrid taste of vomit in her mouth causing her to shudder. She held her side and felt a tear slide out from behind her closed lids.

She felt awful. The night stretched ahead of her, a long dark highway. All she wanted to do was take a painkiller and go to bed for a week. Bloody ovary! Between this one and her non-existent other one, she'd had enough of her female bits and pieces. She pulled off some toilet paper, blew her nose and wiped her eyes. Only eight hours to go.

CHAPTER SIXTEEN

ACTUALLY, Harriet felt better after her quick trip to the loo. The pain was still there but the nausea had settled, and brushing her teeth and a quick splash of water on her face had revived her considerably. She'd only been gone for ten minutes so she doubted whether they'd missed her.

'Here you are,' said Gill, rounding the corner and nearly running straight into her.

'Here I am,' she said, injecting a note of cheer into her voice as she untangled herself from the confines of his arms and kept going.

'How are you feeling? Are you OK? You look a little pale. I looked for you but you'd gone.'

Harriet shrugged off his staying hand on her shoulder, refusing to look into his beautiful grey eyes. She had a night of surgery to get through and if she admitted feeling unwell he would demand she withdraw. Although the thought of it sounded like perfect bliss, she couldn't let the team down.

It was their last day. She'd already had two days out at the beginning of their rotation due to illness when they'd had to operate one person down. They were on the homeward stretch—she would cope with the pain and when it was all over she could skive off.

'Harriet,' he said, grabbing her arm again, and was pleased when she stopped trying to walk away. 'It's bad, isn't it?'

She sighed, still refusing to look at him. If she did that right at this moment, when she was feeling so vulnerable, she was going to cry. 'It's fine,' she dismissed.

He turned her around and lifted her chin so she had no choice but to look at him. 'Talk to me,' he said softly.

She sighed again. 'It's sore.'

'Worse than when you had it drained that time?'

She shook her head, remembering that time vividly. Gill had taken her to the emergency department of the nearest London hospital, doubled up with pain. They'd done an ultrasound and found the large ovarian cyst, and a gynaecologist had done an ultrasonic-guided needle aspiration and sucked off forty mils of serous-looking fluid.

The instant pain relief had been wonderful but short-lived as he'd decided to check out the state of her other ovary and had had to deliver the news about her unusual anatomy. It had been a double whammy on a particularly awful day.

Gill had been great, so wonderful and sympathetic for a while, but as the full implications had dawned on Harriet and her biological clock had roared to life, that's when the arguments had begun.

'No! Absolutely not. It's just a constant ache, more annoying than anything.' She decided not to tell him about the vomiting. 'I'll take a couple of more painkillers. That really knocked it on the head last time.' She turned to go again.

'I really am sorry, you know. About the tube…the whole baby thing. I swear to you, Harry, if I wanted a baby, I would want one with you.'

Harriet stopped in her tracks. She turned to look at him and saw his genuine sentiment written all over his gorgeous face.

'I know, Gill. I know.' And she turned on her heel and headed back to the theatre to help clean up. What was the point in leaving things bitter and twisted? She knew he meant it. She knew he was genuinely sorry about the way things had turned out between them. Her side ached with each footfall and her heart ached with each glimpse, each memory, each breath. Ached for all they could have been.

'You OK?' Katya asked, as Harriet entered the theatre, followed closely by Gill. 'You look pale.'

Harriet rolled her eyes and forced a smile onto her face. 'Looks like I'm going to need to top up my tan when I get home. All this indoors stuff isn't good for you.'

Gill had an instant flash of Harriet sun-baking naked and was glad the phone rang to distract him.

'How did the burr holes go?' asked Kelly.

'Good catch. Large extradural. He's in HDU. He needs evac.'

'I've got a chopper landing in approximately thirty minutes,' said Kelly. 'He can go on that, along with the two abdos Ben's done.'

'I'll ring Megan and let her know to prepare the patients,' said Gill.

'OK, thanks. Now, I've got a middle-aged male with circumferential full-thickness burns to the upper arms. He has cyanosis and impaired capillary refill of his hands, with increasingly weaker radial pulses. He's going to need bilateral escharotomies. His upper chest also has full-thickness burns but they're not circumferential.'

Full thickness meant all of the epidermal and dermal layers of skin had been destroyed and the subcutaneous tissues damaged. 'What's his percentage?'

'I've estimated about thirty per cent.'

'How'd he manage that?'

'In a car that was fired on. It crashed and burned, to coin a phrase. Four others from the same accident are dead, a sixth is arriving soon.'

'Someone's a good shot,' he commented.

'Burns guy also has a deep thigh laceration that'll need a good scrub. Be a sweetie and suture it while you have him under. Reckon you can have it done before the chopper lands? I've organised evac to a specialised burns unit.'

'Slave-driver,' he teased. 'Send it over. What's Ben doing at the moment?'

'Another shrapnel to the gut.'

The already intubated patient arrived within five minutes of the conversation and the team was ready for him. Within ten minutes Gill was ready to put knife to skin.

It wasn't an operation that required a lot of materials. In fact, escharotomies were often performed in ERs and at bedsides with nothing but a scalpel blade. But when you had the use of a theatre and a skilled surgeon, you used them.

Harriet had opened up some drapes, a scalpel and some sponges. For the thigh wound she'd given Siobhan a basic suturing pack and had poured some aqueous chlorhexidine into the metal bowl so the wound could be thoroughly cleaned. The whole procedure shouldn't take longer than twenty minutes.

She turned her back on the patient to start Ella up. She suppressed the shudder she felt at seeing the charred skin. Burns was one injury she found difficult to stomach. Even in the early stages and from behind a mask, they had a smell about them that was very distinctive.

Given the delicate state of her stomach, Harriet decided the further away she stayed, the better. Siobhan shouldn't need anything more opened, and if she did then Katya, who was quite interested in burns due to her younger sister having suffered extensive burns as a baby, could do the honours.

Gill saw Harriet standing back and to the side and smiled beneath his mask. Her dislike of burns was legendary. Not that he could blame her. It wasn't exactly his cup of tea either. He could think of other things he'd rather be doing than cutting into dead flesh, but just having her near, humming to Ella, helped take his mind off what had to be done.

Gill knew he had to make the escharotomy incision through the tight eschar, or dead tissue caused by the burn, into the fat layer below to relieve the pressure of the rapidly swelling tissue beneath. Otherwise the swelling would continue and, with no way to escape, further constrict the blood supply of the arms, compromising the circulation and viability of the limb.

He started on the left arm and made an incision through the eschar, into the deeper, viable subcutaneous tissues. It started at the armpit and followed a mid-lateral line down the length of the full-thickness burn and finished just beyond the demarcation line between burnt and viable tissue. The incision gaped but surprisingly didn't bleed very much.

Gill inserted some sponges to absorb the small ooze and then quickly diathermied a few vessels. He noted the hand pinking up and was pleased that such a small, simple intervention could mean the difference between saving or losing an arm.

He repeated the process on the other limb, with the

same result, and was thankful that the man's chest burns didn't encircle his chest wall, as escharotomies were often required in those situations, too. The tight eschar and swelling tissues beneath could prevent adequate chest movement, hindering breathing, and escharotomies were needed to relieve the constriction.

Of course, this man still had a long way to go yet. He would require extensive debriding of the dead tissue and grafting and many, many blood transfusions. The next weeks would require very specialised management indeed.

Gill moved out of the way so Siobhan could fill the escharotomy incision with SSD cream and dress the burns while he dealt with the thigh laceration. Once the patient arrived at a specialised facility they would have their own way to dress the gaping wounds, but MedSurg standard practice was to fill the incisions with the white meringue-like cream, plaster the rest of the burns with the same stuff, cover the escharotomies with a non-adhesive dressing and then bandage them in place.

Gill helped himself to the suture tray and worked on the gaping thigh wound. The man must have lost an argument with something reasonably sharp in the accident. He was lucky that no major vessels had been cut. The wound was oozing but it was a slow trickle. Gill noted Joan and Helmut checking a bag of blood—the first of many for this patient.

A yawn escaped behind his mask as he attacked the deep wound with the soapy chlorhexedine. It wasn't that late, they'd only been operating for a few hours, but lengthy surgery the night before and then Harriet's early morning wake-up call were beginning to have an effect.

He scrubbed away at the pink tissue, refusing to let his mind go back to the divorce. It was done. Still, he glanced at Harriet hanging back by the wall and couldn't quite believe he was never going to be in an operating room with her again. Even during their separation he'd always known she'd come back, but this time when they said goodbye, he knew it was for keeps.

Gill completed the compound scrub of the wound, satisfied that he'd removed all dirt and foreign matter such as vegetation, gravel and grass. He chose a suture from the selection Siobhan had set out for him and began to sew the laceration together again in layers.

The phone rang just as he was putting the last skin sutures in place. Harriet answered.

'Are you done?' asked Kelly, not bothering with pleasantries.

'Just about,' said Harriet.

'Suspected splenic rupture,' said Kelly. 'He needs a laparotomy, stat.'

Harriet placed her hand over the mouthpiece. 'Spleen,' she said, responding to Gill's raised eyebrows.

'What's Ben doing?'

'Did you hear that?' asked Harriet, talking into the phone.

'Just started an amputation,' Kelly replied.

Harriet shook her head at Gill.

'Fifteen minutes,' he said, pulling off his gown. 'Tell her to send it over.'

CHAPTER SEVENTEEN

SOMETIMES this job was crazy and the team found them-selves rushing one patient out to Megan in HDU and pre-paring for another. They heard the helicopter land as their patient arrived and knew Megan and the others would be grateful to soon have four fewer patients.

Harriet wondered how many more helicopters would land tonight before theirs arrived in the morning. She pushed herself to do her job, despite her tummy feeling more and more like a helicopter had landed inside it and was tearing it to shreds with its blades. The painkillers she had taken before the burns case didn't seem to be having any effect this time.

So she decided to pass on scrubbing this time, even though it was her turn. Katya didn't mind and Harriet promised she'd scrub for the next op, even though she doubted she'd feel like doing it then either, unless she had a miraculous recovery.

Her normal treatment for cyst pain was to take paraceta-mol and rest as much a possible. The pain usually only lasted a day or two and was generally fairly bearable. She could manage it just fine without it interfering too much with her day-to-day life or work. It was a nuisance more than anything. But this was shaping up to be almost as bad as the time she'd had to have it drained.

Great! She didn't want to have to spend her stopover in London having fluid sucked out of her abdomen. Not a great way to start her new life. And Gill wouldn't be with her either…just as well he was heading straight home or she didn't know if she'd be brave enough to go through the procedure alone.

And then what would he think? She was supposed to be ending it, making a clean break. No wonder Gill had been a little surprised by the divorce papers that morning. Talk about giving him mixed signals! She'd been away for a year and had completely caved after being back in the team for one day and had slept with him. And every day since practically, apart from the time she'd been sick.

She had to stop leaning on him. She'd managed for a year without him but had just fallen back into old habits this last two months. No. Gill would go home to be with his grandfather and she would see to her own condition if that was what was required.

Kelly accompanied the patient from the medical building. Theire came also, talking quietly to the young man.

'This guy is the sixth passenger from that car accident. He jumped clear of the vehicle before it crashed and exploded, but landed heavily on his left side. He's complaining of abdo pain and has rebound tenderness in his left upper quadrant.'

'Kehr's sign?' asked Gill, knowing that when blood from an injured spleen irritated the subdiaphragmatic nerve root, referred pain was felt in the left shoulder tip.

Kelly nodded. 'There's free fluid in the abdomen on ul-trasound. He's hypotensive and tachycardic. He's had two units of colloid and that's his second unit of blood hanging.'

'Pain relief?' asked Gill, as he switched on the hand-held ultrasound machine and located the free fluid Kelly had been talking about.

'He's had some morphine. Theire has explained what you're going to do.'

'OK, thanks, Kel. Don't suppose it's slowing down?'

Kelly laughed. 'In your dreams, Guillaume,' she threw over her shoulder as she and Theire exited the theatre.

Gill went to scrub and was surprised when Katya joined him. 'I thought it was Harry's turn,' he said, as he soaped up his hands.

'She didn't want to. She's going to scrub in next.'

Gill hesitated behind his mask as he asked the next question. 'Is she all right, Katya?' He had heard her con-fiding in Katya earlier on—maybe Harriet had told the Russian nurse more about her pain.

'Nothing a baby wouldn't fix,' she said, not bothering to even look at him.

Gill's hands stilled momentarily, before recommencing the scrub. Not really what he'd meant.

'Katya,' he said, a warning in his voice.

'Guillaume,' she said, turning to him, her eyes sparkling with ferocity above her mask. 'You are a stupid man. To think I wasted my affections on you a few years ago.'

Gill smiled and bit the side of his cheek to stop himself from laughing. He should have known that Katya the blunt wouldn't have paid any heed to the verbal stop sign.

'You love her, don't you?' Katya demanded.

'Of course.'

'Then give her what she wants. That's what you do when you're in love. You make the other person happy.'

'She doesn't want that, Katya. I offered this morning. She wants me to *want* a baby.'

'Stupid man,' said Katya, flicking off the tap with her elbow and flapping her arms up and down to shake off the excess water. 'What's not to want?'

She disappeared quickly and Gill, who was stuck with a mental image of Harriet holding Gillian as he washed off his soapy arms, couldn't answer her question.

He followed her into the theatre and noticed that Ella was already playing. Their patient was anaesthetised and Joan indicated she was ready as soon as Gill had gowned and gloved and joined them at the table.

He prepped the area, swabbing it generously with Betadine, streaks of the brown liquid running down the patient's flanks, and then draped the abdomen, leaving the patient's stomach exposed.

With a final nod from Joan he accepted the scalpel from Katya and put knife to skin. The spleen resided in the left upper quadrant, under the diaphragm and lateral to the stomach. It was protected in part by the ribs but despite this it was prone to blunt trauma.

He made a classic incision, a vertical one about twenty centimetres long, over the spleen area. He cauterised the bleeding points as he went, entering the peritoneal cavity and retracting the skin and muscle layers.

There was blood, a lot of blood. He couldn't see anything. 'Suction,' he said to Katya, who put the sucker head into the pool of blood, half filling the litre suction bottle.

'How's he doing?' he asked Joan, without looking up, as he continued to operate.

'A little hypotensive still.'

'There's a hell of a lot of blood here. You may want to rapidly infuse some O-neg.'

Gill approached the spleen from the underside to fasten the splenic artery, fully expecting the dark purple, bean-shaped organ to fulfil the grade five criteria—totally shot. There was too much blood to hope to salvage it and no place in field surgery to attempt it anyway.

This young man needed the haemorrhaging organ removed pronto so his blood loss could be stemmed. Luckily it was a bit like the appendix—not vital to life. Sure, it had important immune and sequestration or storing functions, but other areas of the body could take over the spleen's role easily.

Gill worked methodically to tie off the spleen's blood supply and ligamental attachment. Everything had to be ligated so the organ was no longer fixed to the peritoneum before he could remove it. He had to take special care that he didn't interfere with any of the nearby pancreas's blood supply as he went. In fact, he had to be very careful of the pancreas altogether, given its close proximity.

He shut himself off to everybody and everything except the odd update from Joan and Ella Fitzgerald singing… He forgot about his grandfather and the divorce and Peter and Harriet and that this was their last day. All he could see was moist, bloody tissues, all he could feel were slippery, warm body parts and all he could smell was burning flesh as he cauterised anything that bled. And in thirty minutes he'd removed the spleen.

'Good God, it looks like someone's put it in a blender,' said Helmut, as Gill held it up for everyone to see.

He plonked it in the kidney dish Katya held out for him

and removed the sponges he had packed into the abdomen to soak up some of the blood. He could hear Harriet and Katya doing a count and realised he was back again from the zone he'd been in. He was conscious of things again, noises and activity beyond his immediate space.

He took the opportunity, now that the patient's bleeding was under control and his observations had stabilised, to do a quick exploration of nearby organs. The pancreas, diaphragm and stomach were all examined and found to be intact. Gill explored a little further, checking also on the nearby kidneys.

Satisfied that everything looked good, Gill lavaged the abdomen and closed the muscle and skin layers. The phone rang and Harriet, who was nearest, answered. She nodded as she watched Gill degown.

'Above-knee amputation. Incendiary device,' said Harriet.

'Bring it on,' he said.

CHAPTER EIGHTEEN

2400 HOURS

TWENTY minutes later they were operating again. Harriet was scrubbed in with Gill. She hadn't really wanted to. The pain in her side was getting quite bad but at least with something to do she might be able to keep her mind off the constant throb. And she had promised Katya.

It was going to be a long procedure, probably close to ninety minutes barring complications, and would require all her concentration to anticipate Gill's requirements and keep the operation flowing smoothly. She loved that most about her job. The dynamics of an experienced surgeon and the assistant. Watching people who had been operating together for a long time was like watching prima ballerinas dance *Swan Lake* or a concert pianist playing classical music.

Every move was choreographed perfectly. It was fluid and graceful. One hand meeting the other at just the exact moment to accept an instrument without any interruption to the flow of the proceedings. It was a special skill and talent built up over years, and pure art to watch.

The pain in her side was making it difficult for her to concentrate. She needed to get into the zone that Gill always entered the second he picked up a scalpel. Because if she didn't stay one step ahead of him and he had to wait for something, it would pull him right out of his bubble. And that made him frown and even though he was too polite to say anything, she would know she had let him down and professionally she had never let him down. Never.

Sure, in the beginning there had been an awkwardness to their technique, as there always was with a new partnership. It hadn't been as smooth and the flow had been stilted. Rigid, mechanical even. But she had always managed to anticipate his requirements and the flow soon followed.

Harriet took a deep breath, forcing herself to relax. If she could get outside her body and into her head then, just like Gill, all else but what the two of them were doing would cease to exist. Including the wretched pain!

Gill heard Harriet's indrawn breath, quite loud in their close confines. He turned to her and raised his eyebrows at her, still worried about her abdominal pain. He felt slightly reassured by her quick wink but he noted the fine sheen of sweat on her brow with concern. It wasn't an uncommon sight, given the hot theatre lights directly above their heads, but it was unusual before the op had even got under way.

'I'm good to go,' said Joan.

'Tourniquet on at 0010,' said Helmut, and noted it down on the anaesthetic sheet. The leg's major blood vessels had been crudely ligated in the field as a temporary measure to prevent the patient from exsanguinating through his open wound. It was Gill's job to fix the mess and to do that he needed a bloodless field and haemostatic control of the leg.

A tourniquet was used for this purpose. It could be left on for a maximum of two hours but it was important that it be released about every ten minutes to reperfuse starved tissues and prevent ischaemia, possibly necrosis from tissue hypoxia. The normal rule of thumb was ten minutes on, ten minutes off. It was Helmut's job to control, monitor and document the inflation and deflation of the tourniquet.

Gill looked down at the prepped, mangled right leg. It had been traumatically amputated just above the knee joint, necessitating a transfemoral or above-knee amputation. The flesh was shredded. The distal extremity of the femur or the condyles had been completely blown to smithereens. The sharp splintered edges of the femoral shaft were exposed. An X-ray had revealed no fracture further up the femur.

The missing limb had been completely blown to pieces by the look of the remaining leg and, even if it had been rescued and had been in good enough condition, there wasn't the time and it wasn't the place for lengthy limb salvage operations requiring delicate microsurgery.

Gill looked at the mangled remains of the leg, thinking it looked like some gruesome prop dreamed up by a special effects department. War injuries necessitating amputation were very different to nice clean civilian jobs, the majority of which were performed electively for vascular problems. In combat wounds the initial trauma usually involved a high-energy impact, completely shattering bone and severely damaging soft tissue.

The nature of these wounds required a staged-management approach and were left open until the soft tissue had recovered and stabilised. They were also exceedingly dirty and attempting to close the wound too early could result in failure and infection, requiring a higher level of amputation.

Gill's immediate job was to get the bleeding under control and prepare the muscles, nerves and bone for closure at some stage down the track. And evacuate him to the nearest specialist facility. These centres were equipped to deal with traumatic war injuries. Through aggressive wound care and physio, they would optimise recovery of the injured tissues and eventually close the skin, fashioning a stump that a prosthetic device could be fitted to.

The first thing Gill had to do was decide on the level of amputation. Most surgeons incised about fifteen centimetres above the knee joint but each case was individual and traumatic amputation often required a higher amputation level to allow for viable skin and muscle coverage of the bone.

Gill made his transverse incision about twenty centimetres. It was well up from the mangled tissue and jagged bone edge and Gill estimated there would be enough healthy skin to cover the stump. The tourniquet provided a perfectly bloodless field, enabling Gill to keep going without having to use diathermy on any bleeding points.

He was aware only of the leg and Harriet's presence beside him. She wasn't humming as she usually did, but Gill couldn't think of a better person to be in the zone with. She passed him up instruments as if she'd been born to it. The pain obviously wasn't affecting her ability to assist him and he drew comfort from that.

Harriet made a supreme effort to concentrate on the operation. Gill was proceeding through the muscle layers, dividing the nerves as he went so the cut ends would retract below the end of the remaining bone. This was important to help with the phantom limb pains suffered by most amputees.

She did a quick mental check that everything Gill would need or ask for after this stage was on the tray and within easy reach. Orthopaedic sets were just a big boy's tool set. The instruments weren't dissimilar to what you would find in any home toolbox—saws, chisels, hammers, screws, drills and nails.

Oh, sure, they had more sophisticated names but looked almost exactly the same. Harriet found the bone crunching and sheer force required in a lot of orthopaedic ops unsettling. It was kind of brutal and she guessed you just had to have the Y chromosome to get it.

The pain had become stabbing now and Harriet felt the hot, sharp jab in her side and shut her eyes briefly. She opened them again, forcing herself to tune it out and concentrate on what Gill was doing. There was a long way to go yet, and she would not let him down.

The clock ticked by as Gill took care of vessels, ligating them. There was relative silence in the theatre, apart from Ella, and Gill occasionally enquiring about their patient's condition from Joan.

Harriet reflected how the in-theatre dynamics were different to their out-of-theatre dynamics. Their team chatted and joked a lot outside Theatre. They were close and revelled in banter. But on the job it very much depended on the type of surgery and the pressure Gill was feeling.

If Gill felt relaxed enough to be chatty then everyone followed suit. But this sort of surgery by its nature was intense, performed on critical patients, and they all felt the enormity of the responsibility they had to keep the patient alive. They followed Gill's lead. If he was quiet then they all knew and respected his skill enough to let him work in peace without distraction. If he wanted to joke and chat, that's what they did.

The clock was just about to tick over to the next hour when Gill said, 'Release the tourniquet please, Helmut.'

The tourniquet deflated slowly and Gill watched the operative site carefully for any bleeders. A couple of little vessels oozed and Gill achieved hemostasis with them quite quickly, not bothering to ask for the tourniquet to be reapplied. The tissues were pinking up now as the blood flowed back to them and Gill didn't want to compromise the circulation to the amputated limb any longer than he had to.

Harriet picked up the Gigli saw for the next stage of the operation—cutting the femur. An intense, stabbing pain kicked her hard in the side with breathtaking ferocity and the saw slid from her fingers, dropping with a loud metallic clatter to the floor as she clutched the operating table for support.

An instrument dropping in Theatre pealed as loudly as a church bell. Everyone started and stopped what they were doing.

'Harry!' said Gill, turning. 'Are you OK?'

'Of…course,' she said weakly, swallowing a wave of nausea. 'Sorry, it slipped.'

Gill kept looking at her, searching her eyes, wishing he could see all her face to see if she really was OK. Harriet had never dropped an instrument in all the time they'd been operating together.

'I am allowed one slip-up in seven years, aren't I?' she asked defensively, to his incredulous look. And to buy some time to get her breath back from the suddenness of the fierce pain.

'Siobhan, I'm sorry, can you sterilise the saw again?'

Siobhan picked it off the floor at her feet and took it outside to run it through the three-minute sterilisation process.

'Are you sure you're OK?' asked Gill. 'Do you want Katya to scrub in?'

'I'm fine,' Harriet dismissed as the pain returned to a more intense throb. She'd never not seen an op through to the end, and she wasn't about to start.

CHAPTER NINETEEN

THERE was a delay while the saw was being resterilised. Gill was out of the zone now and the silence was a little awkward so he encouraged Helmut to tell them a joke. Helmut was very good at jokes with just the right sense of drama to deliver the punch line well. He also had an endless supply and was just what they needed right at that moment.

Harriet laughed weakly with everyone else at a one-armed surgeon joke, blinking hard to clear a wave of dizziness that threatened to unbalance her. She opened her eyes and was pleased to see the furniture that had been swimming in front of her eyes was firmly back on the floor.

Siobhan returned with the newly sterilised instrument, placing it on Harriet's trolley. Harriet passed it to Gill, without dropping it, and the procedure got back on track. She glanced at the clock on the wall as she shifted from foot to foot in her rubber theatre clogs, trying to work out a stance where the pain was more tolerable.

Thirty minutes, she thought. Tops. All she had to do was last till the end of this procedure and then she would retire unwell, more casualties or not. She didn't like letting the team down but this pain was only intensifying, and just getting through this op was going to be hard enough.

She just wanted to get off her feet, take some more painkillers and curl up in bed for a while. Although she might ask Joan if she could run the hand-held ultrasound over her abdo first just to confirm it was a cyst. Harriet was beginning to become a little concerned by the ferocity of the pain. What if it wasn't an ovarian cyst? What if she was brewing an acute case of appendicitis?

That'd be a pretty horrid way to end a very eventful last day. She hadn't been looking forward to the end of her rotation here—too many permanent goodbyes to be said, too much history coming to an end—but now it couldn't come fast enough.

Gill started to saw through the femur and Harriet shuddered as she suppressed another rush of nausea. The sawing noise wasn't much different from sawing through wood but just knowing it was human bone lent a certain gruesome quality to the procedure. In fact, watching a mangled piece of leg being sawn off a body did have a certain Frankenstein ghoulishness about it.

After some furtive position changes, Harriet worked out a stance that minimised the pain. She half leaned on the operating table for support, enabling her right foot to be raised off the ground slightly so there was no weight being applied down through her right side at all. The pain was still there but the intensity was less and until the operation was over that was going to have to do.

Gill approached the bone-shortening stage of the operation with great caution. If he got the length wrong, it could set the patient's recovery back. And if he didn't smooth the end of the bone properly, uneven prominences could be damaging to surrounding tissue, cause pressure and irritation and even make it too painful to wear a prosthesis.

His goal was to be quick, but everything he did now was going to count when the next lot of surgeons came to complete the patient's surgery. He had to get the basics right now so it didn't complicate any further surgical procedures.

He sawed it level with the incision line, knowing that the bone had yet to be smoothed, which would shorten it a little further. The femur needed to be shorter than the muscle and skin flaps that the next surgeon would construct to cover the raw end of the bone. The muscle flaps would be sutured over the bone and then the remaining flaps of skin would be sutured together to make the stump.

Gill fussed around with this part of the operation for about half an hour and Harriet shifted off her right leg again and tried not to scream. Not even the soothing tones of Ella helped. Yes, Gill was just doing the best job for his patient, checking and double-checking that the muscle and skin would adequately cover the bone. And then not being totally satisfied that the raw end of the bone was as smooth as it could be and asking for the rasp once more so he could smooth it further.

She blinked as a bead of sweat ran into her eye and she gripped the table as a surge of dizziness made her sway a little. She could feel the threatening nausea and didn't know how much longer she could stand there for. Something was very wrong. The pain in the last ten minutes had kicked up another notch. It felt like someone had stuck a hot, sharp knife into her side and was twisting it back and forth.

This was now much worse than the time she'd had her cyst aspirated. Was it much bigger this time or had it ruptured? Or was it something else? She'd never had appendicitis and if it was that, had it ruptured? The knife twisted again and Harriet suppressed the moan that sprang to her lips.

'Harry? Harry? Did you hear me?' Gill turned to look at her.

Harriet blinked, shaking the fog out of her brain, and the two Gills she could see merged into one.

'Dressing. We're done here.'

Harriet almost cheered as, with shaking hands, she passed him a non-adhesive dressing to place on the open wound. Lifting the stump so he could wrap a bandage around it took a supreme effort. Her arms felt like they couldn't support a leaf, let alone half a leg, but she gritted her teeth, biting down on the sob that almost escaped as stretching across the table caused the knife to twist again.

'Higher,' said Gill, trying to wrap the last of the bandage down the thigh to anchor it a little.

Harriet heard his voice from far away as a ringing in her ears grew so loud it was like being in the middle of a million crickets. Her arms shook uncontrollably and her vision blackened from the edges in until all she could see were two pinpoints of light and then not even that. She felt rather than heard the cry of pain escape her lips before she lapsed into unconsciousness.

Gill realised what was happening just in time, dropping the almost bandaged leg with a thump and twisting to catch Harriet before she banged her head on the floor. Luckily he didn't need to be sterile any more because he ended up on the floor beside her.

'Harry! Harry!' he said, shaking her, ripping her hat and mask off, alarmed at her rag-doll limpness. He heard her moan and saw her eyes flutter open briefly, and felt such a surge of relief she was alive he almost kissed her.

'What's wrong?' demanded Katya. Everyone had gathered around and were squatting next to Gill, their patient temporarily forgotten. The look of alarm and concern on their faces spoke volumes about their feelings.

'She fainted,' said Gill, laying her head gently against the floor and calling her name.

Harriet came round slowly and then was ripped suddenly out of the warm haze by the stabbing pain in her abdomen. No, she panicked, she wanted to go back into the dark hazy place. It hadn't hurt there. For a few blissful moments the pain had ceased to exist and it had been pure heaven.

She moaned and sobbed and brought her legs up so she was lying in a foetal position, her arms folded across her aching stomach. She slowly became aware of her dearest friends and colleagues all peering anxiously at her.

'Joan, can you reverse the anaesthetic on our one-legged friend and get him out to Megan so we can put Harry up on the table?'

The team sprang into action. Joan injected the reversal agent and the patient came round quickly. The four of them helped to shift the groggy amputee onto a trolley and Helmut and Joan wheeled him in to Megan as Siobhan and Katya cleared all the operating debris and wiped the table down quickly.

Helmut returned quickly and he and Gill lifted Harriet off the floor and placed her on the table.

'What happened?' he asked Harriet, alarmed by her pallor as he wrapped her arm in the blood-pressure cuff attached to the anaesthetic monitor and pushed the button. Her skin felt cool and clammy and he tried to stay calm. Joan clipped a tourniquet on her other arm and flicked the prominent vein in the crook of her elbow, ready to insert an IV.

'The pain's been getting worse and worse, Gill,' she said, tears running down her cheeks.

'Why didn't you say something?' he chided gently.

'I just kept thinking, It's only a cyst, it's not going to kill you. But I don't know, Gill. This is different. I think maybe it's ruptured or I have appendicitis.'

'Where does it hurt?' he asked.

'Same place, but it's never been this bad. Not even that time in London.' Harriet unfurled herself with great difficulty so Gill could examine her abdomen. He lifted her top to expose her abdomen and pushed down gently with his fingertips in the right lower quadrant, using the prominent jut of her hipbone as leverage.

Harriet cried out and clutched his sleeve.

'I'll get the hand-held,' said Katya.

The blood-pressure reading pinged onto the screen. Eighty-five systolic and her heart rate was one hundred and twenty.

Katya arrived back and handed the portable ultrasound machine to Gill. He flicked it on, applied some gel and ran the transducer over the suspect area. Harriet groaned and tried to push the transducer away, guarding the tender area. It was hard to get a decent view because Harriet was combative and not letting him push hard enough, but he could see an alarming amount of free fluid and flicked a quick, worried glance at Joan.

He located the ovary and it looked normal. It wasn't her appendix either. He thought he could see an irregularity in her Fallopian tube and felt his heart sink. A problem tube, extreme pain, hypotension, tachycardia and a lot of free fluid added up to only one thing.

He took a deep breath to calm his racing heart, which was thudding so loudly he almost thought there was another helicopter landing outside. 'Harry, are you pregnant?' He switched off the machine and passed it back to Katya.

Harriet looked at him, trying to compute what he'd said. 'W-what?' She shook her head. 'What do you mean?'

'I mean I think you have an ectopic pregnancy that's ruptured your Fallopian tube.'

She stared at him, her foggy brain making it difficult to process what he was saying. Pregnant? She was pregnant? But what…? How? It didn't make any sense. She was on the Pill…

'Harry, I need to operate. You need a laparotomy.'

'No,' she said, placing her hand protectively over her abdomen. 'No.' And burst into tears.

CHAPTER TWENTY

GILL shut himself down. Hardened himself to Harriet's tears. If he didn't do something pronto, she was going to die.

'Let's go, people. There's a lot of blood. Joan, let's get another line and rapidly infuse some O into her. Are you right to do the anaesthetic?'

'Of course. What about you? You shouldn't be operating on Harry. I can get Ben.'

'No. He's in the middle of his amputation.'

'You can swap,' she said gently.

He shook his head vehemently. 'We don't have time. I'm it. I'm doing it.'

Joan looked at the determined jut of his jaw and nodded silently.

Harriet sobbed harder as they talked around her, the true implications dawning. She'd been pregnant and now she wasn't. And there was no time to ponder the details or grieve over a baby she had never known about. Ectopic pregnancy was the highest cause of maternal death in the first trimester of pregnancy. If it had ruptured, she was bleeding—seriously. She could die.

If it had ruptured and she survived, then she'd probably never be able to conceive again. It just wasn't fair.

She clutched Gill's arm. 'Promise me you'll try and save the tube, Gill. Promise me. Don't take away any chance I have of having a baby.'

Gill shut down all the feelings and all the questions he had crashing around in his brain. Right now he had to be a surgeon first and a husband second. 'Harry, I love you. I will try but you know…' He shook his head.

'Just try,' she begged, her face screwing up as she choked on a sob. 'Please, Gill. Please.'

He looked at the woman he loved and all he could feel was the frantic reality of her situation. He had to stop the bleeding or she would die. Her request shouldn't even rate, but her desperation clutched at his heart. He could be the one responsible for taking away her already reduced fertility and deny her the one thing she wanted more than anything. More than him. More than their marriage.

'I'll try,' he said, and walked away to scrub.

The next few minutes passed in a blur as Helmut placed a mask on her face and connected her up to the monitor. She couldn't stop crying. Even among the hustle and bustle all around her and amidst some of her dearest friends, she felt totally alone.

'I'm going to put you to sleep now, Harry,' said Joan gently.

Harriet blinked as Joan's blurry face appeared above her. 'No, wait, Joan,' said Harriet, pulling her mask off, desperate to garner more support. 'Swear to me you'll remind Gill of his promise.'

'Harry…' said Joan, torn between Gill's surgical duty and her friend's grief.

'I will keep him to it,' said Katya, her head appearing in view now as well, as Joan replaced the mask. She was scrubbed so she was standing well back from the edges of the table, her gloved hands clasped together and in close to her body.

'Thank you, Katya,' whispered Harriet, more hot tears pouring from her eyes. She wanted to link hands to touch her friend and convey her gratitude, but even in this warm and fuzzy state she knew Katya was sterile and therefore untouchable.

'It's time,' said Joan gently.

Harriet nodded and swallowed another lump of emotion rising in her chest that threatened to overwhelm her. She pulled the mask off again. She knew that things were touch and go with her and that she might not pull through. She didn't want to leave without them knowing.

'I love you guys,' she said in a voice she had to force to be loud, a single tear squeezing out from the corner of an eye. She didn't have the energy for grand speeches but at least she'd said what she'd needed to.

Everyone paused for a moment at Harriet's words. Gill's step faltered as he entered the theatre. Joan stopped in mid-check of the laryngoscope. Helmut looked up from preparing drugs and Siobhan and Katya stopped their count. Every one of them knew what was on the line. They knew that Harriet's life was hanging in the balance.

Gill recovered first. 'Let's go, people,' he barked tersely.

The team resumed their duties. Joan injected the milky anaesthetic agent into Harriet's IV and Gill watched, relieved, as her eyes drifted shut and the muscle relaxant smoothed the lines of anguish on her face. Joan then inserted the long metal blade of the laryngoscope into

Harriet's mouth and Gill looked elsewhere. He couldn't stand to watch her being intubated. A procedure he'd seen a thousand times, a necessary requirement for surgery, but he just couldn't bear to see it. It suddenly seemed brutal instead of necessary, and the thought of the woman he loved undergoing such a procedure was more than he could bear.

Siobhan cut Harriet's scrubs away, preserving as much of her modesty as possible, and Gill prepped her abdo with Betadine and then quickly draped her body. He couldn't stand to see her lying there so exposed. Harriet was comfortable with her nudity, sure, but this wasn't a beach. It was a cold operating theatre in a strange country and these weren't random strangers, they were her friends and colleagues.

When he looked back at Joan she had completed the intubation and Gill swallowed hard as she taped Harriet's not quite closed eyes shut. The large plastic tube protruding from Harriet's mouth and tied to her beautiful face looked so gruesome, so mechanical.

She didn't look like Harriet, his wife, his lover any more. Harriet, who he had made love to only that morning. Harriet, who had thrust the divorce papers at him. She looked pale and thin and small and...ill. He felt an edge of desperation rise in him and a moment of panic at all the possible adverse outcomes.

He thought back to all the complicated operations he had performed over the last ten years. This was so simple in comparison, a lot simpler than the amputation he'd just performed, but the stakes had never been higher.

Trying to mentally prepare himself for what he was about to do, he understood why surgeons weren't allowed to operate on relatives. The crush of emotions crowding his head and filling his chest made concentration impossible. And what if he failed? What if he couldn't stop the bleeding and she bled out? What if he couldn't do what she'd asked him to do? What if he couldn't save her tube?

Suddenly he wished Benedetto was doing the operation instead. That Harriet's life and fertility weren't his sole responsibility. He wished he could just pace up and down the corridor outside and be free to worry and think the worst. He couldn't think the worst now. He had to do his best, his very best, and that was all he could think about. He was it. It was his responsibility.

Ella started to sing 'I've Got You Under My Skin' and he rejected it immediately. 'Turn if off, Siobhan,' he snapped. He didn't mean to be so terse but it was their song. His and Harriet's. He had proposed to her with it playing in the background and they had danced to it at their wedding. He couldn't bear to hear it now, not when her life hung in the balance.

'Go, Gill,' said Joan.

He didn't need to be told twice. 'Scalpel,' he said, and Katya passed it to him.

He took a deep steadying breath and made a midline vertical incision from below her umbilicus straight down to her pubic bone. He thought how she would now for ever have a scar and wondered if that would prevent her from nude sun-baking.

His hand shook slightly as he made a smaller vertical incision in the fascia and then lengthened the fascial incision, using scissors. He could see the rectus muscle and used the scissors to separate it.

Below was the shiny peritoneal lining and he used his gloved fingers to make a small opening in it near the umbilicus and then used the scissors to lengthen the incision. The object was to be able to view the entire uterus but there was blood everywhere and nothing but Harriet's viscous red life force could be seen.

Gill almost swore out loud, shocked at how much there was even though he knew ruptured tubes bled profusely. This wasn't a surgical emergency for no reason. Oh, dear God! Don't die, Harry. Please, don't die.

'Suction,' he said, knowing that his urgent voice sounded panicky but he couldn't see a goddam thing and he needed to clear it so he could clamp the arteries. He tried to control his panic as the continuous welling of blood slurped down the suction tubing and spat into the bottle, filling one and half filling the next. And he tried not to think the worst as he manually removed the clots and tissue too large to go down the sucker.

He tried to divorce himself from the grisly facts and failed. The fact that her blood loss was frightening and the tissue he was touching was the remains of a tiny, tiny embryo. His embryo. His baby. And he could do nothing. Nothing.

Suddenly he had flashes back to Nimuk's mother. Her abject misery as she had handed Nimuk over, knowing he was dying and knowing there was nothing she could do about it. He remembered identifying with how awful it must have felt for her to be totally powerless, and as he delved inside Harriet he truly understood her despair.

'What's her pressure?' he demanded.

'Holding at eighty. She's had two lots of colloid and just finishing her second bag of O.'

He had to stop the bleeding. 'Bladder retractor.'

Katya handed him the instrument and he placed it, anchoring it on the pubic bone. She also handed him a self-retaining abdominal retractor and he placed that, giving him a good view. He inserted moist towels to absorb the remaining blood and pack off the bowel and omentum from the operative field.

He located the Fallopian tube and his heart sank. He swore quietly behind his mask as he placed two clamps on the destroyed Fallopian tube between the uterus and where the ectopic had erupted, instantly stemming the haemorrhage.

In a theatre where the atmosphere was so tense that no one even dared breathe, his expletive sounded quite loud.

'What?' asked Katya, crowding him to get a closer look.

She repeated his expletive and stepped away. She knew that Gill had no hope of repairing the mangled tube. It looked like a mini-explosion had occurred, shredding the middle of the tube completely.

Gill looked at it helplessly. He doubted whether the most skilled gynae microsurgeon could have done anything with it. He had promised Harriet he'd try, but there was no way anything could be done.

The clock ticked loudly in the silent room. Everyone waited for Gill's next move. After a few minutes Joan said gently, 'We know you'd repair it if you could, Gill. There's not a surgeon in this world that could save that tube.'

'It's her only one,' he said, raising anguished eyes to Joan. 'She wants a baby. I promised her.'

'No,' said Katya, opening Gill's hand and slapping a scalpel into it. 'You promised her you'd try, and I promised her to keep you to it. And if I thought there was any chance, I would. But there's nothing you can do. Cut it, Gill, and get on with the op.'

He'd never felt more out of depth in his life. It wasn't

something he was used to feeling in an operating theatre. Here he was in control. Always. He looked at Joan.

'Katya is right. She's lost a lot of blood, Gill. Don't prolong the stress to her system. There are other ways to get pregnant.'

Gill nodded, knowing they were right but hating himself for what he was about to do. This was why there was a rule about operating on relations and he understood it much better now. He was the one who was going to have to face the music for what he was about to do, and she was going to hate him for it. Harriet hating Ben would have been much easier to cope with.

He hesitated briefly before slicing through the tubal pedicle between the two clamps he'd applied earlier. And that was it. There was no going back now. It was done. Gill pushed all thoughts of Harriet's reaction aside. The deed may have been done but there was still more work to do.

He ligated the artery and then ligated the end of the pedicle. Before he could remove the tube completely, he had to divide the mesosalpinx, the part of the broad ligament that attached along the length of the tube. He clamped, cut and ligated along the length of the tissue until the tube was finally free.

Katya held out a kidney dish and Gill discarded the mangled flesh. It looked alien. So removed from its actual function and too damaged to do it anyway.

'Keep it,' he said to Katya. Maybe Harriet would need proof, justification as to why he hadn't tried to salvage it. Maybe for her grief process she'd need to see it with her own eyes.

She looked at him for a long moment. *'Da.'* She nodded and indicated to Siobhan to get her a specimen container.

'Pressure rising. One hundred systolic,' Helmut said.

Gill felt an enormous weight rising off his shoulders. They had done it. He had controlled the bleeding and Joan had replaced Harriet's blood loss to stabilise her blood pressure. He felt a cramp in his shoulder muscles and along his jaw and realised he'd been tense the entire operation.

He lavaged the peritoneum with warmed saline, thoroughly rinsing off any blood and clots and tissue. 'Let's close,' he said, satisfied at the clear fluid being sucked into the tubing.

As he sutured Harriet back together, his mind began to wander and he forced himself to push the thoughts away and concentrate. He would have time later to think about how close he'd come to losing her, about all the blood and how he'd taken from her the one thing she'd asked him not to.

And that Harriet had been pregnant with his child. A child that he hadn't even known he'd wanted. Until tonight.

CHAPTER TWENTY-ONE

'NO, I CAN'T take it, Kelly. My rotation here finishes in three hours and I want to be there when Harriet wakes up. How far is Ben off finishing?'

'Approximately thirty minutes.'

'How stable is he?'

'OK, for now.' The knife, still gruesomely *in situ,* appeared to have missed anything major according to the X-ray. 'It's been well padded and supported so it can't move around.'

'Sedate him,' suggested Gill. 'He should be fine as long as the knife remains stabilised. What else is there?'

'That's it for now. We've had mainly medical and minor surgical cases from this skirmish. How's Harry?'

'Still sleeping.'

'I'll be over to see her when I can. Are you OK?'

'No. Not really. It's been a hell of a last day.' And that, thought Gill, was an understatement. Divorce papers, his grandfather's poor health, a helicopter shot out of the sky, Nimuk, seven hours of operating and Harriet.

'New team is scheduled to land at 6 a.m. Not long now.'

Three hours away, thought Gill as he replaced the phone in Megan's HDU/recovery area. It stretched ahead of him. He'd rather evacuate Harriet now, but he knew she was stable and their scheduled flight wasn't really that far off, and taking the place of a critical patient wasn't good medicine.

He wandered back over to the bed where Harriet lay, sleeping off the effects of the anaesthetic. The background battle noises that had been going all night had ceased and it was very quiet in the darkened area, only the sound of monitors and the squeaking of Megan's shoes disturbing the peace.

She looked fragile, like she'd had the stuffing knocked out of her. She was so still and pale. He looked at the drip chamber of the IV, watching the steady drip of dark red blood. She was on her third bag and Gill knew, despite her pallor, that her haemoglobin level, which was ten, wasn't too bad, considering the amount of blood that she'd lost.

It was the sheets, he'd decided. The white, white sheets weren't helping her colour. Odd really because with her olive complexion that tanned so easily, she'd always looked so healthy and glowing in anything white.

He held her hand, careful not to bump the bed or her stomach, and thought back to their wedding day. She'd worn white that day and had looked like a beautiful rare flower. The ceremony had taken place on a secluded beach at an exclusive Fijian resort with just family and a few close friends.

If he thought hard enough, he could almost hear the gentle lap of the waves against the shore as she had walked the short frangipani-strewn distance between the guests. And he could almost smell again the heady fragrance of the sweet flowers. They were the two enduring memories of the day still powerful enough to be almost tangible.

She had worn an exquisite white sarong lightly embroidered with unusual milky pink and grey mother-of-pearl beads. She had been planning on wearing a bright sarong to match his bright hibiscus print silk shirt, but had seen the beautiful garment in the resort shop and hadn't been able to resist it.

And what a bride she had made. She had been stunningly gorgeous. With white frangipani blossoms in her loose, long brown hair and a white frangipani bouquet, she had looked beyond beautiful. She had looked tanned and healthy and glowing and he hadn't been able to wrap his head around the fact that she had actually been there to marry him.

Harriet stirred and mumbled a little, and Gill smoothed her wedding band with his thumb as the memories faded. She'd woken only briefly after Joan had extubated her. She had asked for him then had mumbled and made no sense. She no doubt felt as wretched as she looked, and sleep was the best tonic immediately post-op so he didn't disturb her.

He was overwhelmed though by the urge to crawl in beside her and cradle her against his body. She looked eerily lifeless, despite the steady blip, blip, blip of her heart rate on the monitor beside her, and he yearned for the reassurance that only feeling the thud of her heart against his would give him.

His ragged breath stuttered into the quiet air and he began to tremble as he set free the thoughts and feelings he hadn't allowed himself during the operation. It was only now, after the surgery and being relieved from his duties and watching the even rise and fall of his wife's chest, that the enormity of everything crowded in.

Harriet had been pregnant. With his baby. At least, he assumed it was his. Harriet had told him earlier that there had been no one else. He had believed her then and he believed her now. Which made the baby his. His.

The word reverberated through every cell of his body and his hand trembled as the fact sank in. He waited for the usual feelings of rejection and denial and wasn't surprised to find the idea didn't bother him as it once had. He remembered the moment during the operation when he'd been inside her, truly inside her, and he had panicked because her warm, sticky blood had been everywhere, but despite all that had yearned to see his child.

Gill screwed his eyes shut as a shaft of pain stabbed into his heart. Was this the yearning she had felt for the last couple of years? And why had it taken the death of his child and the near death of his wife to realise how strong these emotions could be?

The ache was too much and he forced himself to concentrate on the hows and whys. The timing fitted with an ectopic pregnancy. Not that he'd been up on her cycle, but if she'd conceived almost immediately it would have put her in the right gestational bracket for a tubal pregnancy.

He knew she was on the Pill, had seen her take it on more than one occasion on this rotation. But there had been those couple of days when she'd been ill at the beginning that could have interfered with the absorption of the contraceptive, leaving her unprotected. She could even have gone on to have a normal period under the influence of the Pill, despite being pregnant, which would explain her obvious confusion when he had told her the news.

So he didn't believe that she'd known and had been keeping it from him, or that she had deliberately got pregnant either. Her vehement rejection of Katya's suggestion supported this and wouldn't she have just told Katya anyway that she was pregnant if she'd known about it? Katya had given her the perfect opening.

No, she had been walking around for weeks with a time bomb in her belly, completely oblivious. His child had lodged in her only Fallopian tube, instead of moving down to the roomy comfort of the uterus, and when it could no longer grow within the narrow confines had met an inevitable end and had almost taken Harriet with him.

Him? Gill stroked her hand and wondered about the sex of the baby. He had a strong feeling it had been a boy, or was that just the male in him? A boy or a girl—it hardly seemed to matter now anyway. Would the child have been like him, tall and lean, or like Harriet, toned and tanned? His laugh or her hip mole? His French-ness or her gypsy-ness?

These were questions he'd never have an answer to now. Questions he'd never even cared about or pondered before. What a child with their blend of genes would look like. He'd been a father ever so briefly, many would consider not at all, but the loss he felt was surprisingly heavy.

He looked at Harriet's pale pink lips and wondered if she'd ever forgive him for what he'd had to do. His paternal instinct had only just kicked in, though her maternal instinct had been active for two years now. Her reduced fertility had caused her a lot of grief and he could only begin to imagine how devastated she was going to be.

'I love you, Harry. I'm sorry,' he whispered, and gently stroked his thumb in a butterfly caress across her mouth. She stirred a little, murmuring something in her sleep, and he quickly withdrew his hand.

He knew she would wake up eventually but he was relieved to see her sleeping so heavily. She'd been through so much that she needed it—her body stretched to its limits of pain and blood loss. But also while she slept it delayed the inevitable. He was going to have to tell her the bad news and he couldn't bear to witness her distress when he told her that not only was her baby dead but her ability to have another had been severely compromised.

He felt a hand on his shoulder and looked up to see Katya standing there.

'Did you know?' he asked her quietly.

Katya shook her head solemnly. 'I don't think she even knew.'

He nodded, pleased to have confirmed what he'd already surmised. Katya pulled up a chair on the opposite side of the bed and they watched in silence for a few minutes.

'Don't beat yourself up,' said Katya. 'You did what anyone would have done.'

Gill's gaze didn't leave the rise and fall of Harriet's chest. 'But I'm not just anyone, am I?' he asked.

'There is more than one way to have a baby, no?' she said. 'She still has an ovary. She still has eggs. IVF will help. And if not, you can adopt. Or foster.'

'I know,' said Gill, turning anguished eyes on the Russian nurse. 'But she's still going to be devastated.'

'*Da*. She has lost something very important to her. But as I said, Guillaume, there are other ways and don't forget, you are important to her, too. I suspect as long as you're the father, she'll be OK.'

Gill felt the weight of the shrewd gaze. Too shrewd for one so young. Him, a father. Something that had horrified him a mere few hours ago suddenly appealed immensely. Two a.m. feeds and a diminished sex life didn't seem so sacrificial. Not compared to the very real sacrifice that Harry had just made. Losing her baby and her remaining Fallopian tube.

The pain of losing the little life they had made together seemed to have kicked his fatherly instincts to life. And it had been like rousing a sleeping lion—they were well and truly tripped into overdrive.

A picture of Harriet holding Gillian rose unbidden into his mind and he had to grip the mattress as the desire to see her holding his child almost crushed him.

CHAPTER TWENTY-TWO

0400 HOURS

HARRIET roused slowly, coming out of the layers of fog gradually. Her tongue felt furry and disgusting, her breath tasted bitter in her mouth. The room was blurry and it took a few moments for it to come into focus. She couldn't remember where she was, although it was vaguely familiar.

It certainly wasn't her bedroom in Bondi. She couldn't hear the familiar beat of waves against the shore but Gill was there. She looked down, his head warm against her arm, his eyes shut. She took a moment just to stare at his face, something she'd done often while he'd slept. Although his features didn't seem quite as relaxed as usual. They seemed tense, troubled.

Megan skittered past, adding to the surrealism. Harriet watched her go about her work in a disjointed, puzzled kind of way. Where was she? Was she dreaming? What had happened? There was a dull ache in her stomach and she shut her eyes, sighing blissfully that the pain had gone at last.

And it all came back to her in horrible Technicolor detail. Her eyes flew open. She'd never felt more awake in her life. She tried to sit up, displacing Gill.

'Harriet,' he said, waking instantly, cursing himself for having fallen asleep.

Megan saw Harriet's attempt to sit up and rushed to help her. Harriet desperately wanted to tell her to stop fussing, but she felt as weak as a kitten and knew she was flailing hopelessly about like a drunken octopus. Gill joined in, stuffing pillows behind her back.

'What happened?' she asked. She'd wanted her voice to sound stronger but her throat was sore and her voice sounded hoarse and it hurt to talk. 'The baby…'

Megan's eyes met Gill's and she melted discreetly away.

'Harriet…'

She braced herself. From the time they'd first met he had shortened her name to Harry. He'd only ever called her by her proper name during their wedding vows.

'It was an ectopic. The tube had ruptured. There was nothing I could do.'

Harriet heard the words as if they were coming from far away, but they hit her with the speed and ferocity of a cobra strike.

She couldn't stop the gasp or the rush of tears. 'So, I was…pregnant?'

'Yes,' he said quietly.

Tears streamed down her face and she clasped her hand protectively over her stomach. The unfairness of it all was crippling. The one thing she'd wanted more than any-thing—taken from her before she'd even had a chance to savour it.

She took a few moments to compose herself before she asked the next question. 'What about my tube?'

Gill would have given anything to be anywhere but there right now. He wished he had a magic wand and he could put everything right for her. For them. Bring their baby back. Her tube back.

'I'm sorry,' he said gently. 'I had to remove it.'

Harriet stared at Gill with tear-filled eyes as he blurred out of focus. This wasn't happening. It just couldn't be happening. This just wasn't fair. What had she done to deserve this?

Her despair took hold and she wanted to lash out at him. 'Did you even try?' she demanded, not caring that her voice was loaded with bitterness.

Gill felt the stab of her harsh words and ignored their sting. He'd known this wouldn't be an easy conversation to have. 'It was a mess, Harriet.'

'So you didn't even try? Even though you promised me you would?' Her voice shook and wobbled as the enormity of what he had done really hit her.

He felt her pain as he watched tears run unchecked down her cheeks. 'There was no point,' he said, trying to say it as quietly and gently as possible. 'I—'

She sucked in a breath and wished she had the energy to slap him across the face. 'No point? No point?' she said, her voice rising sharply.

Was it not bad enough that he had removed a vital part of her reproduction capabilities? Did he really have to dismiss it like it meant nothing? Pass it off as some clinical surgical decision with no consequences? 'Speak for yourself.'

Gill cursed in French. 'I didn't mean it like that, Harry…I meant the tube was too damaged to even attempt it.'

'Oh, right,' she said, sniffling and flicking her hair off her face and wiping at the flow of tears with the back of her hand. 'You can spend half an hour getting an amputation just right but you can't give me equal consideration?'

'That's different, Harry…'

'Is it? Is it?' she demanded, not caring that her voice was verging on hysterical or that the pitch hurt her vocal cords tremendously. 'The difference is, Gill, that a stranger's prosthetic future was more important than my future fertility. Because, let's face it, that's hardly on your list of priorities, right?'

Gill could feel his jaw clenching at the unfairness of her verbal attack and took a moment to answer. She was angry and upset, saying the first thing that came into her head, he knew that. But it still hurt.

She continued into his silence. 'I mean, what do you care? Suck out a baby, rip out a tube. What's it's to you? Just one less complication in your perfect, child-free existence.'

Harriet broke off on a sob, lying back against her pillows, and he could hear the anguish in her cries.

'It was my baby, too,' he said quietly.

She raised her head up and fixed him with an angry stare as a harsh, incredulous laugh curled her lips. 'Your baby? Since when have you cared?'

He reached for her hand, to tell her that he did care. That losing a child, no matter how embryonic, had been unexpectedly devastating and a wake-up call to his paternal instincts.

'Don't touch me,' she snarled, withdrawing her hand from his reach. 'Don't ever touch me again.'

He swallowed a lump in his throat as he pulled his hand away. Her distress was painful to watch. She was like a wounded animal lashing out at whoever was closest. And it just happened to be him.

He knew she wasn't being rational and refused to take what she said to heart, but he also knew that trying to reason with her at the moment was folly. The news was too new, too raw. Anything he said now about his new feelings would only be dismissed with a cutting cynicism. She needed some time to digest what had happened, grieve for her baby and her Fallopian tube.

She was sobbing loudly now and he wished he could say or do something to help. It seemed ludicrous to be sitting so near his distraught wife and not be able to comfort her.

'Just go, Gill,' Harriet said between sobs, not even bothering to look at him. 'Leave me alone.'

'No, I want to stay.'

'I don't want you here,' she said miserably, even though perversely every cell in her body wanted to fall into his arms and cry until there were no tears left.

Her rejection hurt but, despite his injured pride, he sensed it wasn't what she really wanted. He looked helplessly at Megan and she shrugged.

'Give her some time,' she mouthed at Gill.

'I'll come back in a bit,' said Gill, rising to leave, feeling completely out of his depth.

Harriet turned on her side, away from him. 'Don't bother.'

CHAPTER TWENTY-THREE

HARRIET lay awake, crying silently into her pillow as a desert dawn broke gently over the harsh landscape outside. Megan came by every now and then to check on her and ask if she needed any pain relief. She refused. The pain was hardly anything compared to what it had been before she'd collapsed. And nothing compared to the ache in her heart and the bruise on her soul.

In fact, she welcomed the vague incisional discomfort. At least it was a reminder that, ever so briefly, she had actually been pregnant. There was nothing else to show for it. No trace that a baby had been growing inside her. Gill's baby. Just the pain and eventually, she supposed, a scar.

Trying to get her fuzzy head around the fact that she'd actually conceived was almost too much in her weakened anaemic state. How could she not have known? She knew enough as a nurse to know that the contraceptive pill wasn't infallible, that there was a small failure rate. But how could she not have *known*?

She'd always thought she would just…know. The minute…the second it happened. That her desire for a baby was so strong, so elemental that she'd be totally in tune with her body's signals. That something inside her would know the exact moment egg and sperm joined and started to multiply.

But apparently not. She thought back to her cycle, trying to work out when she had conceived. The two-day lurgy she had caught initially had probably been the culprit. She'd been about mid-cycle when she'd arrived two months ago so she had obviously ovulated when the Pill's influence had been interrupted because of her illness.

Which meant she must have fallen almost immediately afterwards. She thought back to the time when Gill had knocked on her door the night after her symptoms had abated. She had felt wrung out and had spent most of the day in bed, sleeping. He had spent fifteen hours operating and had looked as done in as her.

But he had made her get up and have a shower and brush her teeth and put on clean pyjamas. You'll feel better, he'd said, and he'd been right. He had changed the sheets for her and brought a tray of tea and a mountain of hot buttered toast and ordered her to eat it. He had made enough for both of them and helped her finish off the entire plate.

He'd also helped himself to her shower and had come out with her towel slung low on his hips and asked her if she fancied some company. Just sleep, he had assured her. They were both exhausted. She'd nodded because he'd been such a sight for sore eyes and she didn't have the energy or desire to turn him away.

And they had slept. For about five hours. But then she had woken to his hand on her hip and his stubble on her shoulder and she had wanted him. And it had been as if he had known, too, because he'd stirred, kissed her shoulder and she had turned in his arms and they had made love. And had been doing it ever since, despite their irreconcilable differences!

She forced her mind away from replaying images of their two months together. It hadn't resolved anything and she'd probably been exceedingly foolish to have ever thought it would. She did a quick calculation to banish the self-recriminations. She must have been about seven to eight weeks along, which fitted the time frame for a ruptured ectopic perfectly.

She gingerly felt her abdomen. It was still so hard to believe. She had been pregnant for almost the entire time she had been here, and hadn't known. There had been none of the usual symptoms newly pregnant women complained of. No nausea, no breast tenderness, no debilitating tiredness, no funny cravings.

If only she had known! But how could she have? She'd had two periods while she'd been here. Looking back, they hadn't been typical—a little lighter and shorter than normal but not noticeably so. She hadn't really thought about it, had put it down to a different time zone, country and climate mucking with her cycle—quite common in her line of work.

Being pregnant had never occurred to her. Never! She knew that you could still have a cyclic bleed if you were pregnant and taking the Pill and could only assume that this was what had happened to her. Why hadn't she questioned a scant period instead of just being relieved and grateful?

She felt the hot sting of tears in her eyes again. It just wasn't fair to learn of her baby and lose it all in the space of two hours. Why couldn't she have had some time to savour the new life growing inside her? To be happy and joyous as all mothers-to-be were? To walk around with the delicious secret like she was the only woman in the world who had ever managed the miracle of new life.

But, then, how would she have handled Gill? Would she have told him or kept it from him? Could she have borne it if he had stuck to his guns and rejected their baby? But what right would she have had to withhold it from him?

Despite her anger at him, there was no other man's baby she wanted more. Despite her insistence that he sign the divorce papers and set her free to find someone else, deep down she doubted she'd ever find another Gill. Another man she could love enough to share the most intimate of human experiences. She had come here to leave her marriage behind, but maybe the invisible hand of fate had had other things in mind.

Maybe it had been her destiny to come back and fall pregnant by Gill. Maybe there was some vital life lesson they were both supposed to learn from these tragic circumstances. Was it supposed to make them see reason? Bring them closer? Because at the moment she had never felt further from him.

They should be together as a couple mourning their loss. She should want him to be by her side, comforting her. And she should be letting him lean on her, giving him a shoulder to cry on. But why would he waste his breath grieving for something he had made patently obvious he had never wanted in the first place?

What had he said—it was his baby, too? What the hell did that mean? She daren't let herself think it was an emotional plea from a man who really cared. It was probably more some macho statement. Staking a claim. Another way to tie her to him.

She was too physically and mentally done in to try and

figure it out. The only important thing was that she'd been pregnant and now she wasn't. Her head hurt and her heart ached and all she wanted to do was cry herself to sleep.

'Harry?'

Harriet shut her eyes hard and lay very still on hearing Katya's voice. Go away. Leave me be. You promised, too, damn it. You're as bad as him.

Katya came round and stood in front of her. 'I know you're awake, Harry, I could hear you crying.'

Harriet reluctantly opened her eyes. 'I'm tired,' she said, fixing her gaze on the neckline of Katya's scrubs.

'You're angry,' said Katya, coming straight to the point in her typically blunt fashion.

Harriet felt tears well in her eyes again and choked on a sob. Yes. She was. But she was hurting deep inside more than anything else.

'Gill did an excellent job. He did everything he could.'

Harriet snorted, not ready to forgive Gill yet. Was he sending others to fight his battles now? 'He didn't even try to repair the tube, Katya. You were there, you know that.'

Katya stood staring down at her for a few moments, the things she wanted to say getting all jumbled up inside her head in a bilingual tangle. Her friends were hurting and she wanted to help get them back on track. To get them to see that they belonged with each other.

She decided showing was better than telling. 'I brought something for you.' She thrust the medium-sized specimen jar at Harriet. The damaged Fallopian tube floated in a clear alcoholic solution.

Harriet looked at the offering but could barely see it properly through her watery eyes. 'What is it?' she asked, grabbing a tissue from the box Megan had left on her table.

'It's your tube.'

Harriet blinked. She slowly reached out and took it from Katya. She gingerly tried to pull herself up into a more upright position, failing badly until Katya took pity and helped.

Harriet blew her nose and wiped her eyes then held the jar up to the light. Oh, dear. What a mess. There was a gaping hole in the middle of the specimen. The slenderest thread of tissue held it precariously in one piece superiorly. The ragged edges of the rupture looked like they'd been put through a mincer and there was obviously not enough tissue remaining to have made closing the shredded edges even a remote possibility.

Harriet felt hot tears rise in her eyes again and the specimen blurred out of focus. Katya took the jar from her trembling fingers and placed it on the table.

'There was nothing he could do, Harry,' she reiterated gently.

'Oh, Katya,' cried Harriet. 'It's not fair. Why me, why me?' Her face crumpled and when she felt the comforting hug of Katya's arms around her shoulder, she completely broke down.

After a while Harriet's distress quieted and Katya handed her the box of tissues. 'I must look an absolute mess,' said Harriet, drying her face again.

'I have seen you look better,' Katya admitted.

Harriet laughed at her friend's candour and felt the strain on her vocal cords. You would never get a big head around Katya.

'Oh, God, Katya,' she said, chewing her lip. 'I was so horrible to Gill.'

'Gill is a big boy. He understands,' she dismissed.

Harriet laughed again and felt it in her stitches this time.

They sat in companionable silence for a couple of minutes. Harriet picked up the jar again. 'I don't have another. What am I going to do, Katya?'

Katya placed her hand over Harriet's. 'There are many ways to have a baby,' she said. 'So, it's not going to be as easy for you as a lot of women out there. So be it. IVF, adoption.' She shrugged. 'You will have a baby, Harry. I just know it.'

Harriet felt the threat of new tears at her friend's faith. She wished she could be so certain. 'It's not such a romantic way to start a new life with someone, though, is it? Marry me and have my babies—you don't mind providing a specimen in this jar do you?'

They both laughed, but it hurt Harriet's stomach, and the thought was so depressing that she quickly sobered. 'What if no one wants me?'

'Gill does.'

Harriet nodded slowly. 'It's not enough. I need more.' She picked up the jar again, inspecting her lost tube. 'This just makes me more determined. For a few weeks I was a mother. I want that again.'

'And Gill was a father. A lot has happened tonight, my friend. You two need to talk. Why don't I go and get him?'

She shook her head. 'He said he'd be back.' Well, before she'd told him not to bother, anyway. Luckily, he didn't insult easily. 'I'm tired and I need some time to think for a while.'

They did need to talk—she definitely needed to apologise to him if nothing else. But the op and the bleeding and a thousands tears had left her drained and weary. She felt like she could sleep for an eternity. Gill could wait.

CHAPTER TWENTY-FOUR

GILL sat on the edge of his bed beside his packed bag. He held his copy of the divorce papers in his hand. He was staring so hard that the words 'irreconcilable differences' duplicated themselves before his tired eyes. Harriet's bitter 'Don't bother' echoed through his head.

He'd had a good hard think about his life since Harriet had asked him to go. He didn't want this. He'd never wanted it, had only signed the damn papers because she'd wanted it. But the events of the last twenty-four hours had made him reassess their supposed differences.

So much had happened in such a short space of time. It was like each thing that had happened had been part of some grand plan, bigger than him, to make him see the error of his ways. Unbeknownst, each wake-up call had given him a piece of a puzzle. A puzzle that he hadn't been able to figure out until all the pieces were in place.

His first wake-up call had been the divorce papers. After two months when he had thought they'd been reconciling, they'd come as a surprise. They'd made him really look hard at the things Harriet had been asking of him over the last two years. And had made him question the strength of his beliefs. Were they really worth losing Harry over?

Next had been his grandfather falling ill. The news that his fit and healthy grandfather had succumbed to a massive heart attack had been a shock. He'd always seemed larger than life, like he'd live for another eighty years. But…he was…old and Gill realised that he'd neglected him over the last decade.

Sure, his grandfather didn't mind in the least, was proud of his humanitarian-minded grandson and encouraged him to continue the aid work. But family was important, too, and it had taken this one last day to make him realise that.

Next had been Nimuk. The baby's death had affected them all but particularly Harriet. Her distress had reached inside and clawed at his gut. But more surprisingly had been the way he'd identified with the mother. Looking at her, mute with grief, had scared the hell out of him. The emotional vulnerability of parents was frightening. A fact that he'd confronted a mere two hours ago when he'd been unable to protect his unborn baby.

And then a really startling wake-up call. The death of Peter Hanley and the aid team, shot out of the sky by the very people they were here to help. It was easy to forget his job was dangerous. Potentially, anyway. He'd never felt unsafe, or rarely anyway, but a tragedy like that brought the safety issue into the spotlight and Harriet's worry about him continuing his work in such areas had made him think more seriously about the dangers.

After that, there had been Gillian. Wake-up call number five. Puzzle piece number five. His reaction to seeing Harriet holding the newborn had been unexpected. Suddenly, out of the blue, he'd been able to see her holding their own child. A child he'd been fighting with her about for two years. A child he'd had no interest in. But he had passed Gillian to her and he had seen the whole fairy-tale. He'd seen what happened after happily ever after. And it hadn't been awful. In fact, it had looked kind of nice.

And then the biggest wake-up call of all. Harriet. Even thinking back now to how much blood there had been and how another ten or fifteen minutes and she could have been dead was unbearable. And knowing that somewhere in all the blood had been the remains of his baby. A child he hadn't even known about, but its embryonic death and having to excise it from her body had left him with a deep, deep sadness. And worse, a gut-wrenching helplessness. The sort he had seen already on Nimuk's mother's face.

And afterwards, when Harriet had been so distressed and angry, lashing out at him because he had done his job, no matter how much he wished it hadn't been his to do. Her angry 'Since when have you cared?' had really hit home.

Since the divorce papers and his grandfather and Peter and Nimuk and Gillian. Since being inside her, her blood everywhere, scared that she could die and feeling so helpless that he hadn't been able to keep his baby safe. He cared. It'd just taken an extraordinary amount of wake-up calls.

But he was fully awake now. Despite being up all night, more awake than he'd ever been. The puzzle pieces had fallen into place. He wanted a baby with Harriet. He wanted to impregnate her. He wanted to watch her flat belly burgeon as it grew inside her. He wanted to deliver it. He wanted to watch her breast-feed. He wanted to bath it and play with it and rock it to sleep. He wanted it all.

And he knew it would be more difficult for them to conceive now. But it didn't matter. Whatever it took. Fertility treatments. IVF. Hell, they'd adopt if conception wasn't possible. But he wanted it all. The whole fairy-tale. The bit that came after happily ever after.

Hang the 2 a.m. feeds and the botched social life and the absent sex life. They'd slept enough hours and they'd gone to enough restaurants and they'd had more sex in seven years than most people had in a lifetime. There was a time for those things and there was a time to settle down and reproduce, and he felt the urge grow stronger with each passing minute.

Harriet had told him to leave her alone. 'Don't touch me ever again,' she had said. But he knew he just wasn't capable of that. Even if they never conceived and were never blessed with a baby, he didn't want to be apart from her ever again. Ever! They had spent one year apart and it had been hell. He wanted to live with her and their children and grow old together. Nothing had ever been clearer.

Not even the moment he'd realised he'd fallen in love with her and wanted to marry her. That had been natural, something where no thought had been required—just human love and lust and emotion. But deciding to stay together, have a baby together, was clear thinking at its best. Despite all the potential problems and hurdles, he wouldn't take no for an answer!

Gill rose from the bed empowered by his decision. He would not leave here without her. The chopper would be landing soon, signalling the end of their time there. He had less than thirty minutes to convince her the child he'd always rejected was now something he couldn't live without.

The divorce papers burnt a hole in his hand as he swiftly navigated the corridors, his big strides purposeful and determined. She was mad but he would make her see reason. She was post-op, he should let her rest and recover her strength, but there was no time for being delicate or gentle. There was too much at stake.

Megan looked startled as he strode into the room but he ignored her. He had eyes only for Harriet's slight form in the bed, her back to him. He noisily plonked himself in the chair beside her bed and was gratified when she fluttered her eyes open. His gaze caught the specimen jar on the nearby table, Harriet's excised tube lying limply at the bottom in all its garish splendour.

He picked it up and said rather abruptly, 'So, you know.'

'Yes,' she said, her voice cracking. She cleared her throat, clutching her neck, wincing as she swallowed.

Gill almost sagged in relief. He knew the experienced theatre nurse in Harriet couldn't look at the specimen and still blame him. Thank goodness for Katya.

'I'm sorry, Gill,' she said in a hoarse whisper. 'I was angry. It's obvious nothing could be done.'

Gill felt tears prick his eyes and blinked to clear them. She sounded so final. So sad and defeated. The righteousness he felt at her admission tempered by her frank sadness. Her eyes were red-rimmed accentuated by her pallor, as if she'd cried herself to sleep, and she looked as if there was no puff left in her sails. So different to the live, vibrant Harry he'd met and married seven years ago. Or even the one he had made wild, noisy love to the previous morning.

He shrugged and said gently as he took her hand, 'You were angry.'

She shook her head. 'I should have known. I know you. I know you would have tried your best. You are a brilliant surgeon, Guillaume Remy. Don't let anyone ever tell you anything different.'

Gill felt his heart swell with love and pride at the humility of the woman he loved. But the finality of her words were worrying.

He stared at her beautiful face for a few moments. 'I have something for you,' he said.

'Oh, yeah.' She smiled lightly and felt her dry lips crack in protest. 'The last time someone said that they handed me a grotesque specimen jar.'

He brought the divorce papers up into her line of vision. She looked at them and looked at him. He held them by the top edge in the middle and slowly ripped them in two. Then in four. Then in eight. And continued until they were almost confetti-sized. Then he threw them in the air and they fluttered down around their heads and on the bed and to the floor.

'No, Gill. No,' she said in horror, as she watched the pieces fall.

'Yes, Harry. Yes.'

Great! Now she was going to have to get new ones drawn up! She glared at him as the last bit fell in his hair. 'That was a legal document.'

'I don't care,' he said. And he didn't.

Harriet was lost for words. She couldn't move on with her life until she and Gill were divorced. His little trick just delayed the process a little more. 'Gill—'

'Shh!' he interrupted noisily. 'Be quiet. I have things to say, Harry.'

Harriet blinked at his forcefulness. She took a moment

in her still foggy brain to comprehend. Before she could rebuff him, he was off again.

'This last day has been hell. My grandfather…Nimuk…Peter…Gillian…you.'

Yes, she thought. As far as last days went, this one had sucked big time!

'But when I was inside you and there was so much blood and I thought I was going to lose you…that was the absolute rock bottom. And I knew in amongst all the blood was my baby. Our baby. And this paternal instinct came out of nowhere and I was sad. I saw you with Nimuk and with Gillian and I knew. I just knew that my destiny was to have a baby with you.

'All the years of denial and arguing just paled into insignificance. Losing our baby was the one thing that made me realise that I wanted to have a baby more than anything. And not any baby, Harry. Your baby. Our baby.'

Harriet watched his sweet mouth move and got confused about what was actually coming out of it. She blinked a few times before her foggy brain actually assimilated the information. It was too much to take in. She felt like he was speaking to her in a foreign language.

Her heart jumped even as her sensible head rejected the idea. 'No,' she said.

'Yes,' he said. 'You told me yesterday that I had to want a baby so badly that my breathing hurt when I thought about it. That my arms ached and my heart felt bereft and my stomach empty at the thought of not having one. You said I had to want one with very fibre of my being. Every cell. And you were right. And I do, Harry. With every cell in my body I want a baby.'

Harriet blinked back tears at the passionate words. But

still she rejected them. 'No, Gill. Even if I believe what you just said, what about your job? Your career? I won't subject my child to a part-time father.'

'I don't want to be a part-time father, Harry. I want to be a hands-on, completely doting father.'

Harriet brutally clamped down on the part of her that was foolishly rejoicing. 'No. You don't.'

OK, this was going to be difficult. 'Yes. I do.'

'Gill,' Harriet sighed, letting out the breath she had been holding, one that had expanded as her crazy mind had run off with the possibilities Gill had filled it with. 'OK, you lost a child tonight.' Her voice was surprisingly strong but she knew what she said next would be vitally important. 'And you had a big scare. But you're a brilliant surgeon and sooner or later you'll get itchy feet and want to be amongst it all. And you should be. This is what you do best. You'd end up hating me, Gill. I don't want to be married to a man who resented me.'

'This is what I love, Harriet, but there are plenty of things I can do closer to home that help. I've been neglecting my family. Grandfather's heart attack made me realise that while I've been gallivanting around the world, I've barely had time for them. My parents, my grandfather, they're not young any more. I can go into administration. Vic has been trying to lure me into MedSurg management for years.'

Victoria Johnston, the Australasian director of MSAA, had been wooing Gill for a long time. She had seen him as the perfect candidate to manage the different surgical programmes. She'd wanted someone with grass-roots experience, who could troubleshoot and see the bigger picture prior to sending teams in at ground level.

Harriet was horrified. 'A desk job? No, Gill. No. You'd hate it!'

'Actually, no,' said Gill, already thinking about the possibilities. The things he could change and implement to make things easier for the teams on the ground. 'It'd be a challenge.'

Harriet shook her head, feeling like bursting into tears again. She wanted him to want a baby, but not like this. 'What about surgery, Gill?'

'What about it?' he said, grinning at her madly. Suddenly, after a vile twenty-four hours, things were looking up.

'Won't you miss it?'

'Probably after a while. But there are plenty of aid programmes in Australia for the disadvantaged, where I can work if I feel the pressing need to have a scalpel in my hand again.'

'But how long will it be, Gill? Realistically? Before you feel the need to be in the thick of things again? I wouldn't want you to ever go to another war zone. Ever. There are plenty of ways you can die in a safe place like Australia. I couldn't bear being at home with our child, waiting for you away in some hot-spot, praying that no one would shoot your helicopter down or hold a gun to your head, demanding you treat them first.'

He kissed the back of her hand and smiled at her gently. 'You're not listening, Harry. My days of hot-spots are over. I've given ten years and as exciting as it's been I'm ready for the next chapter of my life. I want to go home. I want to be a father.'

Harriet regarded him seriously for the first time. She couldn't believe what she was hearing. She could hear the sincerity in his voice and see it on his face. But it just didn't seem possible after two years of persuasion, arguing and tears.

She felt her eyes water and then a single tear track down her face. 'This would be a really bad time to screw with my head, Gill. Don't say stuff like this if you don't mean it. Really mean it, deep down. Or even if there's a single skerrick of a doubt tucked away anywhere in your body.'

He smiled at her, wiping away the tear with his index finger and trailing it down to brush lightly against her lips. 'I love you, Harriet Remy. I have never felt more sure of anything.'

Another tear spilled over and followed the first one. The irony of the situation was incredible. After two years of resistance Gill was ready to have a family, just when her ability to have one was in doubt. 'What if I can't have a baby? What if I can never have a baby?' she croaked, the thought of it so devastating her voice cracked.

'We'll adopt or foster or…get a surrogate or…I don't know. I don't care. But we'll do it, Harry. I promise you, we will have a baby.'

'What about the sleepless nights?' She sniffled.

'Bring them on.'

'And the non-existent social life?'

'Can't wait.'

'And feeling too wrung out to have sex?'

Gill paused. 'Don't care,' he dismissed with a boyish grin.

'Oh, Gill,' she cried, her face crumpling as her heart leapt with joy. 'Please, tell me I'm not hallucinating,' she sobbed.

He laughed and kissed her, tasting the salt of her tears. 'I'm not a mirage,' he said, kissing hard on the mouth again. 'You are not hallucinating. My name is Guillaume Remy. I love you and I want your baby.'

She held out her arms and he very gently leaned in towards her, laying his head against her chest, accepting her embrace. He heard her sigh and knew they were both back where they belonged.

The noise of a distant helicopter's rotors approached and he looked up into her face. 'That's our relief team. Come back to Australia with me?'

Harriet nodded through another wave of tears. 'I love you, Gill. I'm never leaving your side ever again.'

'Good. It was hell without you.'

She laughed and hugged him close to her again. He was right, it had been hell. And the last twenty-four hours had been a cram-packed roller-coaster of emotions that she never wanted to experience again. But they were staying married. They were going to have a baby. And if it had taken losing a baby and losing her ability to have any more, ultimately it had been worth it.

She absently brushed a piece of divorce-paper confetti out of his hair and looked up into her husband's loving grey eyes. It was so lucky, she thought hazily as his mouth came down on hers, that their differences had been reconcilable after all.

0906 Gen Std HB

MILLS & BOON®

Live the emotion

OCTOBER 2006 HARDBACK TITLES

ROMANCE™

The Christmas Bride *Penny Jordan*	0 263 19246 6
Reluctant Mistress, Blackmailed Wife *Lynne Graham*	
	0 263 19247 4
At the Greek Tycoon's Pleasure *Cathy Williams*	0 263 19248 2
The Virgin's Price *Melanie Milburne*	0 263 19249 0
The French Count's Pregnant Bride *Catherine Spencer*	
	0 263 19250 4
The Billionaire's Marriage Mission *Helen Brooks*	0 263 19251 2
The Christmas Night Miracle *Carole Mortimer*	0 263 19252 0
The Millionaire's Reward *Angie Ray*	0 263 19253 9
The Bride of Montefalco *Rebecca Winters*	0 263 19254 7
Crazy About the Boss *Teresa Southwick*	0 263 19255 5
Claiming the Cattleman's Heart *Barbara Hannay*	0 263 19256 3
Blind-Date Marriage *Fiona Harper*	0 263 19257 1
A Vow to Keep *Cara Colter*	0 263 19258 X
Inherited: Baby *Nicola Marsh*	0 263 19259 8
A Father By Christmas *Meredith Webber*	0 263 19260 1
A Mother for His Baby *Leah Martyn*	0 263 19261 X

HISTORICAL ROMANCE™

An Improper Companion *Anne Herries*	0 263 19057 9
The Viscount *Lyn Stone*	0 263 19058 7
The Vagabond Duchess *Claire Thornton*	0 263 19059 5

MEDICAL ROMANCE™

The Midwife's Christmas Miracle *Sarah Morgan*	0 263 19096 X
One Night To Wed *Alison Roberts*	0 263 19097 8
A Very Special Proposal *Josie Metcalfe*	0 263 19515 5
The Surgeon's Meant-To-Be Bride *Amy Andrews*	0 263 19516 3

0906 Gen Std LP

Live the emotion

OCTOBER 2006 LARGE PRINT TITLES

ROMANCE™

HISTORICAL ROMANCE™

MEDICAL ROMANCE™

MILLS & BOON®

Live the emotion

NOVEMBER 2006 HARDBACK TITLES

ROMANCE™

The Italian's Future Bride *Michelle Reid*	0 263 19262 8
Pleasured in the Billionaire's Bed *Miranda Lee*	0 263 19263 6
Blackmailed by Diamonds, Bound by Marriage *Sarah Morgan*	
	0 263 19264 4
The Greek Boss's Bride *Chantelle Shaw*	0 263 19265 2
The Millionaire's Pregnant Wife *Sandra Field*	0 263 19266 0
The Greek's Convenient Mistress *Annie West*	0 263 19267 9
Chosen as the Frenchman's Bride *Abby Green*	0 263 19268 7
The Italian Billionaire's Virgin *Christina Hollis*	0 263 19269 5
Outback Man Seeks Wife *Margaret Way*	0 263 19270 9
The Nanny and the Sheikh *Barbara McMahon*	0 263 19271 7
The Businessman's Bride *Jackie Braun*	0 263 19272 5
Meant-To-Be Mother *Ally Blake*	0 263 19273 3
Falling for the Frenchman *Claire Baxter*	0 263 19274 1
In Her Boss's Arms *Elizabeth Harbison*	0 263 19275 X
In Her Boss's Special Care *Melanie Milburne*	0 263 19276 8
The Surgeon's Courageous Bride *Lucy Clark*	0 263 19277 6

HISTORICAL ROMANCE™

Not Quite a Lady *Louise Allen*	0 263 19060 9
The Defiant Debutante *Helen Dickson*	0 263 19061 7
A Noble Captive *Michelle Styles*	0 263 19062 5

MEDICAL ROMANCE™

The Surgeon's Miracle Baby *Carol Marinelli*	0 263 19098 6
A Consultant Claims His Bride *Maggie Kingsley*	0 263 19099 4
The Woman He's Been Waiting For *Jennifer Taylor*	
	0 263 19517 1
The Village Doctor's Marriage *Abigail Gordon*	0 263 19518 X

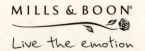

1006 Gen Std LP

MILLS & BOON®

Live the emotion

NOVEMBER 2006 LARGE PRINT TITLES

ROMANCE™

The Secret Baby Revenge *Emma Darcy*	0 263 19014 5
The Prince's Virgin Wife *Lucy Monroe*	0 263 19015 3
Taken for His Pleasure *Carol Marinelli*	0 263 19016 1
At the Greek Tycoon's Bidding *Cathy Williams*	0 263 19017 X
The Heir's Chosen Bride *Marion Lennox*	0 263 19018 8
The Millionaire's Cinderella Wife *Lilian Darcy*	0 263 19019 6
Their Unfinished Business *Jackie Braun*	0 263 19020 X
The Tycoon's Proposal *Leigh Michaels*	0 263 19021 8

HISTORICAL ROMANCE™

The Viscount's Betrothal *Louise Allen*	0 263 18919 8
Reforming the Rake *Sarah Elliott*	0 263 18920 1
Lord Greville's Captive *Nicola Cornick*	0 263 19076 5

MEDICAL ROMANCE™

His Honourable Surgeon *Kate Hardy*	0 263 18891 4
Pregnant with His Child *Lilian Darcy*	0 263 18892 2
The Consultant's Adopted Son *Jennifer Taylor*	0 263 18893 0
Her Longed-For Family *Josie Metcalfe*	0 263 18894 9
Mission: Mountain Rescue *Amy Andrews*	0 263 19527 9
The Good Father *Maggie Kingsley*	0 263 19528 7